Dishes

# Dishes

## RICH WALLACE

VIKING

VIKING
Published by Penguin Group
Penguin Group (USA) Inc., 345 Hudson Street, New York, New York 10014, U.S.A.
Penguin Group (Canada), 90 Eglinton Avenue East, Suite 700, Toronto, Ontario,
Canada M4P 2Y3 (a division of Pearson Penguin Canada Inc.)
Penguin Books Ltd, 80 Strand, London WC2R 0RL, England
Penguin Ireland, 25 St Stephen's Green, Dublin 2, Ireland (a division of Penguin Books Ltd)
Penguin Group (Australia), 250 Camberwell Road, Camberwell, Victoria 3124, Australia
(a division of Pearson Australia Group Pty Ltd)
Penguin Books India Pvt Ltd, 11 Community Centre, Panchsheel Park, New Delhi – 110 017, India
Penguin Group (NZ), 67 Apollo Drive, Rosedale, North Shore 0632, New Zealand
(a division of Pearson New Zealand Ltd)
Penguin Books (South Africa) (Pty) Ltd, 24 Sturdee Avenue, Rosebank,
Johannesburg 2196, South Africa

Penguin Books Ltd, Registered Offices: 80 Strand, London WC2R 0RL, England

First published in 2008 by Viking, a member of Penguin Group (USA) Inc.

1  3  5  7  9  10  8  6  4  2

LIBRARY OF CONGRESS CATALOGING-IN-PUBLICATION DATA
Wallace, Rich.
Dishes / Rich Wallace.
p. cm.
Summary: Nineteen-year-old Danny spends an eventful summer in Maine, looking for romance,
working as a "straight" dishwasher in a gay bar, and trying to reconnect with his estranged father.
ISBN 978-0-670-01139-1 (hardcover)
[1. Fathers and sons—Fiction. 2. Dating (Social customs)—Fiction.
3. Homosexuality—Fiction. 4. Maine—Fiction.]  I. Title.
PZ7.W15877Di 2008
[Fic]—dc22
2007052572

Printed in U.S.A.    Set in Minion    Book design by Sam Kim *for Sandra*

# Dishes

# 1

## "You know . . . *men.*"

I figure Jack must be getting low on glasses, so I head out of the kitchen. It gives me a chance to check on the Yankees–Boston game.

The place is still busy, and half the people are wearing red-and-blue Red Sox caps, including the guy sitting at the bar next to Arnie. I get a lot of shit from the regulars for rooting for the Yankees, but what do you expect? I grew up twenty minutes from the Bronx.

I clear the empties and look at the TV. The Sox are up 4–3 in the eighth, but the Yankees have two men on and Quesada is batting.

"Looks like your boys are in trouble," I say to Arnie. "Quesada's been hitting .400 for the first three weeks of June. With power, too."

Arnie is an older guy—at least sixty, always in a suit jacket and one of his pastel shirts. "We'll see," he says, sipping his wine.

Quesada takes a pitch and the camera zooms in on his scowl. He paws at the batter's box with his foot.

"He's like *this*, you know," Arnie says with a smirk.

I turn to him and he hangs a crooked index finger, letting it flop around like a minnow.

It takes a second for me to catch on to which body part he's imitating. "How would you know?"

"Locker-room rumors." He lets out a short, wheezy laugh. "Steroids will do that to you. Big muscles up top, shriveled ones down where it counts."

Quesada hits a weak pop-up to short, and the inning's over.

"Not much power there," Arnie says triumphantly. "Looked a little . . . impotent, if you ask me."

I laugh. My eyes meet Arnie's date's, a new guy I haven't seen around before, probably half Arnie's age, drinking the house specialty—a cranberry martini. He's got buzzed, blond-tinted hair under the Sox cap and a bunch of tattoos, and he's wearing a black tank top that shows off his weight-room muscles. That macho look is something you're more likely to see over at the Lighthouse or Captain Pete's. (Not that I've actually been to those places, but I see the crowd going in and out and hanging on the sidewalk after hours.)

Our bar—Dishes—draws an older, "sophisticated" crowd: teachers and realtors and business owners. You get some of the lobstermen and mechanics in here, too, but not a lot of them.

Jack grabs my arm. "This kid bothering you, Arnie?" he jokes.

"Oh, no, except for that horrid New Jersey accent. He can stick around me all he wants."

Jack is frenetically chewing gum. He looks over Arnie's shoulder at two men who just came in and flicks up his eyebrows questioningly. "What'll it be?" His voice has a smoker's hoarseness.

He nods and draws two beers, setting them on the bar.

Jack looks at me and points at Arnie. "Tell you what," he says, "I don't have a gay bone in my body, but if I ever did, this is the guy I'd want to hook up with. What you got, a Bentley, a Mercedes, and a sixty-five Mustang?"

"Sixty-seven."

"Same as your age?"

"Not quite."

Jack looks at me again. "The guy spends his summers here and winters in Freeport. Not a bad racket, huh?" He walks to the other end of the bar to refill some drinks. I look at Arnie.

"Pretty cold up in Freeport, no?"

"Oh, God, not *that* Freeport." He puts one hand over his eyes and shakes his head. "Not that god-awful L.L.Bean outlet town. Freeport in the *Bahamas.*"

"Oh."

"If you ever want to visit, just say the word. I'm there all winter." He stands up from the bar stool. "Need a smoke," he says, and they go outside, leaving their drinks and a small pile of cash on the bar.

Jack is in his zone, engaging in conversation with all twelve people at the bar while filling the waiters' orders, never missing a pitch from the baseball game, and managing to amuse, insult, and flatter everyone.

I go back to the kitchen and grab another load of glasses that just ran through the dishwasher. I bring them to the bar, then go back to finish up.

The kitchen's closed; I'll be out of here in twenty minutes. The bar stays open until one on weeknights. I look out the doorway and see Hector carrying a tray of empty glasses toward the kitchen.

Hector looks even younger than me, but he must be older. At least twenty-one, since he serves alcohol here. He has tanned skin and dark hair—short and gelled—and a tiny earring. He's an inch or two taller than me and very lean, wearing sandals and shorts and the dark-blue T-shirt all the waiters wear. It says DISHES: OGUNQUIT, MAINE.

He flits around the room all evening, delivering drinks and pub food, stopping by the tables every few minutes to ask, "Is everything still really delicious?"

Hector makes a lot of money in tips. Big surprise.

He walks into the kitchen, picking a cherry tomato out of the salad he's been working on for at least an hour. He grabs a bottle of dressing and asks me, "Is this nonfat, Danny?"

I shrug. "I have no idea."

He wrinkles his nose. "I don't eat *any* fat. Except cheese. I mean, how can you not eat *cheese*?"

Is that a real question or a rhetorical one? *I* don't eat cheese. Can't stand it. But he wouldn't know that, would he? He's always trying to talk to me. Flirt with me, I mean.

Anyway, have I described enough stereotypically gay men yet? Let's see: the aging, worldly, heavily cologned retired business-man; the desperately-trying-to-look-younger biker/surfer type; the pretty, prissy, effeminate schoolboy. On weekends we've also got a strong lineup of handsome, fortyish, showtune-singing dramatists around the piano bar upstairs, and some of the spillover from the wilder, up-from-Boston-for-the-night crowd that tends to travel in packs and usually frequents the raunchier places across the street. (They're known around here as Massholes.)

We get straight icons, too. The other night the Southern Maine Chapter of the International Women's Club of New England was upstairs, belting out the score of *Oklahoma* with Lance and Alan and the rest of them. And there are always straight couples nursing European beers at the tables, watching the singers and feeling so hip and Democratic with their tolerant, liberal attitudes.

But the truth is that I meet a lot more people here who don't fit any stereotype.

My father, for example: Jack the bartender. Thirty-eight, still trying to look cool, noticeable white hairs in his goatee. He did spend two weeks in the Bahamas last winter. Visiting a friend, he said. And even though I'm living with him for the first time in my life, he's basically as absent as ever.

I run the last few glasses through the dishwasher and wipe down the kitchen counter.

Hector takes off his little white apron and pulls out a wad of bills and starts counting. There's a drop of sweat running below his ear, moistening his olivey skin, and I'm tempted to wipe it away but I don't.

"Good money tonight?" I ask.

"For a Wednesday," he says with a sigh. He gives me a half smile. "Better than washing saucepans."

I shrug.

"When you hit twenty-one . . ."

"I know. That's not till next summer." I won't even be twenty until August.

"I was doing your exact same job a year ago," he says. "Anything to be in Ogunquit. Waiting tables has its drawbacks, but I'm cute, I know it. . . . *You* would make a ton of money."

"Would I?"

He nods, raising his eyebrows a bit. "You have to put up with a lot. You know . . . *men*."

"That bothers you?"

He makes a scolding sound with his tongue against his teeth. "Straight people have this idea that we're attracted to every guy we see. Believe me, I haven't been attracted to *any* of the clientele in here."

"Then what's the appeal of Ogunquit?"

He rolls his eyes. "The ocean. The restaurants. The *men*. Just not these men, particularly. The older ones scare me a little. They tip big, but all a lot of them want is a boy to play with. I'm not some whore. I'm *selective*."

He leans against the counter while I sweep the floor. I look over and catch his eye, and he averts his gaze. I know he watches me sometimes. And he made a point of saying that he's not attracted to the *clientele*.

I have runner's legs and a decent upper body—lots of push-ups and ab work. And I'm running about eight miles a day, including sprints on the beach, so I'm very fit right now.

Hector folds his arms and yawns. "Guess I should go out there and see if I overlooked any money," he says.

I yank my grungy T-shirt over my head—it's greasy and soapy and so is my hair—and put on my spare one that says MORRIS-TOWN STATE TRACK. I sniff the used shirt, which stinks, and hang it in the bathroom for tomorrow.

I slip out the back door while Hector's in the bar room.

So what do you do on a Wednesday after midnight if you're not old enough to go to a bar?

The night is bright and I'm nowhere near sleepy, so I walk past the darkened shops and turn toward the Marginal Way, the footpath that twists above the rocks for a mile or so along the surf, which crashes and froths just below.

I'm not used to all that mental bombardment you get in a bar; I'm at my most centered when I'm working out at top effort. Then when I crash at night—physically exhausted but still sort of wired—that's the only time I'm wishing I had someone to relate to. Someone who could relate right back to me with muscle and energy and release.

I walk through the grounds of the Sparhawk resort and turn to follow the Marginal Way. Here at the beginning, the drop is steep where the ocean meets the Ogunquit River. The tide is low tonight, so the river is at its narrowest, just a fast-running channel maybe thirty yards wide. At high tide it spreads out and covers nearly the entire beach.

The moon is up and the sky is clear, so I have no trouble

following the path. I break into a run, making the sharp uphill turn at the point and winding past the Beachmere Inn and the first of the little rocky coves.

The path turns left, then another hard right, and I run straight into two tightly clenched women walking toward me.

I bounce off the larger one's breasts—big round things about at my eye level—and step back. The words UMASS SOFTBALL are stretched across them. The other woman is shorter and not quite as chunky. They laugh.

"Sorry," I say.

"No problem," says the bigger one. "Kind of late for a work-out."

I nod. They stand apart from each other and look me over.

"I wasn't really working out," I say. "Just unwinding a little."

"Yeah. Us, too," says the other.

"You play for UMass?" I ask.

"We did. We graduated a couple of years ago." She looks at my shirt. "You run for Morristown?"

"Did. But the bastards dropped track."

"Tough break."

"It sucks."

They've moved close together again, and the bigger one has her arm around her partner. "Well," she says, "we won't hold you up."

"No problem," I say, and I start running again.

Frustrating dynamic here by the sea: the men want me, the women want each other. But I've only been here a couple of weeks. Haven't done any true exploring of the possibilities.

I stop at the highest point on the path and take a seat on one of the benches. Like most benches along here, it has a nameplate; this one says DONATED IN MEMORY OF SARAH LITTLEFIELD. Even the wooden garbage bins along the Marginal Way are labeled with platitudes like TRUTH and CHARITY and TOLERANCE.

There are lobster-trap floats bobbing in the water, and you can see lighthouses up in Wells and down the coast in York. If it was daylight, I'd get off the path and make my way along the shoreline on the rocky cliffs.

Daytime in summer this path is mobbed with tourists, but after midnight I'm pretty much alone out here. I like it that way, most of the time.

But before summer gets too old, I'd like to share a night like this with somebody.

# 2

## "A seven-letter word for *masculine*."

I wake up at nine. Jack apparently didn't come home again. I sleep on the couch, so I would have heard him. I've been here two weeks and haven't spent much time with him.

Just like the first nineteen years of my life.

I didn't think I'd come up to Maine and have to fend for myself all the time. But experience should have told me to expect that. Most of my friends have had their fathers around to kick them in the ass when they screw up, or to offer some out-of-touch but sincere advice. Jack's attention span as a father is short-lived, but you'd think the guy would at least take a weak stab at parenting now that he finally has the chance.

The apartment is on Shore Road right in the heart of things, above a T-shirt shop that also sells kites, newspapers, and beach towels. We have half of the second floor of an old clapboard house, with a tiny deck off the kitchen overlooking an outdoor café in the back.

I pull open the sliding door and smell the thick gray porch paint, which never quite dries in this summer humidity. There aren't any fresh cigarette butts in the ashtray on the plastic table, more evidence that Jack hasn't been here. He only smokes outside since I arrived.

He tried to be around, more or less, when I was younger, coaching my Little League teams and taking me to the movies or the Jersey Shore once in a while on weekends. He was seventeen when my mom got pregnant, and neither one of them had a clue what to do about me. So I lived with her and her parents until earlier this month, when I decided I needed some independence.

Jack had started spending a couple of weeks in Ogunquit every summer, then moved here full-time a few years ago. So I hadn't seen him in a couple of years, but he always said I should come up for the season. So here I am.

I eat a nectarine, getting juice on my bare chest, and put on my running shoes.

I start work at four, and I like to run before it gets too hot. We've been hitting the nineties all week, but with the constant breeze from the ocean it never feels too uncomfortable.

I have a loop that takes me up Route 1 for a couple of miles, past all the motels and down along the beach, then finally along a short stretch of the Marginal Way, dodging past couples with baby strollers and sightseers with binoculars and mobs of senior citizens from the bus tours that stop in Perkins Cove.

Midmorning like this, you see lots of young waitresses walking to work in ponytails and shirts with restaurant logos. As I'm running up the hill back toward town, I spot one that I've made eye contact with once or twice. Her white polo shirt has a lobster stitched over her left breast and the words PERKINS COVE HADDOCK SHACK. I run past her every day about this time.

Today she looks up and gives me a hint of a smile. I slow down as I pass and glance back and see that she has an exceptionally nice butt. Tennis player or soccer, perhaps?

"Hey," I say.

She stops walking and brushes a strand of hair from her eyes. "Hi."

It's the most positive response I've had in a long time. From a girl, anyway.

"You work there?" I ask, pointing to the logo on her shirt.

She rolls her eyes slightly. "No. I just like wearing this same shirt every single day."

I notice that she gives me a quick head-to-toe perusal, sort of like Hector does. I'm just wearing shorts and running shoes.

"They got lobster rolls?" I ask.

"Do you know any place in Maine that *doesn't* serve lobster rolls? Even McDonald's has them." She turns her head toward Perkins Cove, then looks at her watch.

"So, you work at eleven or something?" I ask.

"Yeah."

"Okay, well . . ." I point toward town. "I'm, you know—"

"Okay. See ya."

"When?"

"Excuse me?" She gives me a look as if I've just said something stupid.

"You said, 'See ya.' I said, 'When?'"

She gives a short, huffy laugh, aimed right at me. But then she smiles. "Maybe in your dreams."

"I better take a nap then. Prolong the moment."

"Whatever you say," she says. "I'm late."

Shore Road gets way backed up all summer as it approaches Route 1, which is just two lanes and is the main street through Ogunquit. I run past young women in halter tops and guys on motorcycles and in sports cars, plus landscapers in pickups— tanned and muscled with their shirts off—and trucks delivering beer and seafood to the restaurants. They've all got something going on this summer; everybody in town seems to give off this sexual heat.

Like that Haddock Shack waitress. Sizzling. I'll have to track her down again tomorrow.

I see Arnie walking his little beagle, Caruso, along the brick sidewalk, so I stop to pet him.

"Nice coat," I say, meaning Caruso's, not Arnie's. Arnie's is an ugly sky-blue windbreaker.

"It's from the baby food," Arnie says. "He gets puréed chicken every morning. It makes the coat softer."

Arnie's one of the few people I know up here, so I drag out the conversation. "On your way to get a coffee?" I ask.

"Eventually. When he's ready. He walks me all over town first."

"See you tonight?"

"You might," he says. "I might stop in."

He stops in every night and spends at least two hours. But at least he's got a social network. I've got the dishes and my workouts and not much in between.

I spot my father at an outdoor table at Fancy That—Sox cap on backward, large coffee in a cardboard cup, intently reading the newspaper. Probably the horse-race entries at Suffolk Downs. He's chain-smoking and making notes on the paper, looking a lot older than he is. He's got his phone on the table; he keeps glancing at it and picking it up. Jack never stays still for more than a second.

I could ask him where he slept last night, but he never grills me about where *I've* been. Not that I've been anywhere.

He looks up and smiles, and I see that he's actually been doing the *Boston Globe* crossword puzzle.

"What's up, Danny?" he asks.

"Nothing much. Just finished running."

"Ouch. How far?"

"An hour."

He screws up his face like he's in pain. He's not the workout type—just one more thing we don't quite get about each other. Jack has no idea how hard I train and no idea why.

He points his thumb toward the coffee counter. "You want anything?"

"Nah. I'm dripping wet. I gotta shower. I think we still got some orange juice at home."

"Do we?"

"Last I looked."

He nods. "I'll be over in a little while. Didn't get there last night."

"I noticed."

He winks. "Something came up."

"Yeah, like every night?" I thought there'd be some reconnection between us this summer, but so far we're barely even roommates. You'd think he'd care enough to check in on me, at least.

He ignores my annoyance. "Anything 'coming up' on your end?" he asks.

"Like what?"

"Women? Men? It's summer, my friend."

"All I do is work." And I'm not his friend; I'm his son. "Men? You gotta be kidding me."

He clicks his pen about a dozen times in quick succession, then asks me if I know a seven-letter word for *masculine*.

"This a joke?"

"No. It's for this puzzle. Ends in *-ish*."

"*Mannish*, I guess."

"That has two *n*s?"

"Think so."

He starts filling in the letters. "That works."

You need to be pretty confident to do a crossword puzzle in pen. Especially if you can't spell all that good.

"See ya at home or whatever," I say. "I gotta do some push-ups and shower and eat."

"Yeah. Me, too," he says, talking with a cigarette hanging out of his mouth. "Except that push-up part. Sounds too much like exercise."

"That's the other thing I do."

"I know. You might wanna loosen up."

"What do you mean?"

He spreads his hands a bit and looks from side to side, indicating, I guess, that it's a big town with lots going on.

It's a tiny town, in fact, and what's going on here doesn't really involve me.

He gestures to the chair beside him, and I take a seat. He leans toward me and keeps his voice low. "If you can't get laid in Ogunquit, you're not trying very hard."

Now *there's* a wonderful parental message. "Is that why I'm here?"

"That's why we're *any*where, Danny. Take advantage."

I doubt any of my friends have ever heard quite that kind of advice from their dads. But I guess Jack can only relate to me guy-to-guy, rather than father to son. So I play along. "I'm working on it," I say.

"Work harder."

Screw this. "I suppose if I *was* getting laid, I wouldn't have to worry about you walking in on us." I say it sharply. He catches on this time, and his tone begins to match mine.

"So what do you want from me?" He rubs out the cigarette and looks toward the street. "I bring you up here, give you a place to sleep, stock the refrigerator, and don't hassle you worth a shit about anything. When I was your age, my old man used to be on my ass about *every*thing. He'd sniff my jacket whenever I came in to see if it smelled like pot."

"Did it?"

Jack smiles and turns to face me. "Of course it did."

"And what'd he do about it?"

He shrugs. "Threaten me. Act like he was gonna smack me. Meaningless crap like that."

"Sounds like he cared."

He blows out his breath and looks scornfully amused. "There's a big difference between caring and controlling."

Yeah, but either one would be preferable to being ignored.


I pull my sheet off the couch and fold it up and toss my pillow in the closet, then hang my wet running shorts in the bathroom. I lived with a slob in a dorm room last school year and I've had enough of that.

I had a decent cross-country season, then was doing all right in track when they announced that they were dropping the program. Something about not being in NCAA compliance with equal athletic opportunities for women. So instead of adding women's volleyball or something to increase opportunities, they "equalized" things by dumping wrestling and track to screw the men.

I finished the semester, but my attitude turned to shit.

So life was kind of sucking in New Jersey, and I didn't figure Maine would be any worse.

I might spend a year at Coastal Maine Community College

while I figure out what to do next. That would mean living in Ogunquit, of course, since Coastal is strictly a commuter school twenty miles away. I'll need a car, too.

I suppose I could stomach being here awhile. I hear the winters are tough, but New Jersey's no tropic, either. Sleeping on a couch and not having a bedroom door to shut for that long will suck, but Jack's only around so much anyway. He spends January and February tending bar in Florida. He doesn't seem to have any meaningful connections—no steady girlfriends that I've known about, not much contact with his own parents, no friends other than acquaintances at the bar and the racetrack.

By the time I've showered, there are people eating at the courtyard café below the deck. I can smell grilled steak and hear murmurs of conversation. Frank Sinatra music is playing in the background, and ice is clinking as a waiter fills water glasses.

We have no phone other than Jack's cell and no TV or Internet. He's got a shelf of books—Stephen King and John Grisham, mostly—and stacks of magazines on the kitchen table that include *Sports Afield*, *People*, and *Rolling Stone*. There's also the June issue of *Scientific American*, and I have no idea how that wound up in the pile.

He's got a Little League team photo from ten years ago stuck on the refrigerator: me kneeling in the front row in a blue-and-yellow uniform, Jack standing in back, not looking much older than I am now. Why that one, I wonder? My mom's got photos of me all over the house—school portraits, sports shots, candid stuff. All he's got is one meaningless picture?

I turn on the radio (we do have one of those), which is tuned to a classic rock station from down in Boston, which basically alternates songs between Aerosmith, AC/DC, and Pink Floyd, which drowns out the Sinatra from downstairs.

Lunch is a can of tuna fish and another nectarine. We always eat good at work, so there's no need to break the grocery budget at home.

I could survive on nectarines.

Jack survives on caffeine and nicotine.

I probably have the makings of a poem there, with all those words that rhyme.

I just need one that rhymes with *frustration.*

# 3

## "These ones died on the boat."

Fitch, the owner/manager/chef, looks up from the grill around five fifteen and stares at me.

"What?" I ask.

"You want to earn a little extra tonight?"

I shrug. "How?"

"Hector needs to take care of something for an hour or so. We're not busy yet, but what do you think of helping in the dining room? Just putting out silverware and pouring water?"

"Yeah. Why not?"

Fitch is the only person in Ogunquit who knows that Jack is my dad. Jack thought it'd be easier on me at work if no one else knew. I guess he figured it'd be easier for me to hook up with somebody, too.

Fitch goes into his office and tosses me one of the blue DISHES shirts. "Put this on. You can keep it if you want."

I take off my greasy shirt and put on the new one.

Fitch isn't any older than Jack, and in fact he looks quite a bit younger. But he's owned this place for a couple of years. He's usually gone by nine, letting one of the younger cooks handle things from there. Seems to be a good businessman. Could stand to lose some weight.

"You'll still have to wash the pots and stuff," he says. "I'll tell Hector to help you out some if it gets slow later."

"No problem."

Jack gives me one of those "What is *this* all about?" looks when he sees me in the blue waiter's shirt carrying a pitcher of water. I ignore him and fill the glasses at one of the tables.

None of the regulars come in this early. There's a straight couple at the bar with martinis and four older people at a table by the window. One beefy, youngish guy in a filthy shirt and a stained Celtics cap is at the other end of the bar, both hands around a glass of beer.

Jack is slicing lemons and rotating his shoulders to the jazz coming from the speakers.

There's really nothing for me to do out here. Kyle, the other waiter, has it all covered. People don't tend to want dinner in here until much later. The early eaters stampede to the Lobster Pound or the clam shacks on Route 1.

"You need anything?" I ask Jack.

He shakes his head. "Nah. We're all set. Going to get hectic in a little while, guaranteed."

The guy in the Celtics cap nods at me.

"Just get out of work?" I ask.

"Yeah. Long day."

"You work on a lobster boat or something?"

"No. I fix cars." He takes a sip of the beer, which must be one of the imports because it's half empty but still has a thick, foamy head. He talks in a flat monotone, staring straight ahead. "My roommate, he's a lobstah-man."

When a guy mentions a "roommate" in Ogunquit, you usually assume they're sharing more than living space. This guy doesn't fit any type that I've come across, but you never know. Maybe they're just sharing expenses.

"You get a lot of free lobsters, then?"

"A few. He brings dead ones home sometimes and we eat them." He finally makes eye contact with me. His accent isn't as strong as some of the locals, but he does turn his *r*s into *ah*s. "Don't eat a lobstah that's been dead for any while, like if you find one lying on the dock. These ones died on the boat."

"I'll keep that in mind, but I usually eat mine already prepared. In lobster rolls." I pick up the pitcher and take a step toward the kitchen, but he keeps talking.

"Watch out," he says. "There's places in town that make their rolls with frozen meat from Canada. You can tell. Lobstah that's been frozen picks up the taste of the brine it's packed in and gets dry."

"Why would they use frozen meat when we got a whole ocean full of lobster a hundred yards away?"

He shakes his head slowly. "They don't want to do the work

of steaming 'em and breaking out the meat. And getting rid of the waste. The bettah joints would nevah cheat like that, but the places that cater to the tourists . . . some of them are lazy. They're the ones that use a lot of mayonnaise and chopped onion in the mix."

He points his chin toward the people by the window. "The busloads of senior citizens from Pennsylvania don't know the difference, but anybody from around heyah could tell with one bite."

"Thanks for the tip," I say. "How's the Haddock Shack?"

"Down in Perkins Cove? Very good." He takes a longer sip of the beer. "No problem theyah."

Sounds like a second great reason for me to stop by.

It gets insanely busy later in the evening, especially with the piano bar open upstairs. They've got their own bartenders up there and another guy washing plates and glasses by hand (it's a limited menu upstairs—flatbread and wraps), but all of the food is generated down here, and I scrub all the pots and pans and cooking utensils. So I'm still at it way after midnight, which will probably be the norm now that summer is officially here.

Hector's been in and out of the kitchen all night, trying to help by stacking plates or wiping down the counters.

"I feel bad you had to fill in for me," he says. "It was a family thing, a phone call to my grandmother." But he was only gone about forty-five minutes and, like I said, it was quiet the whole time. It didn't set me back any.

I notice that he's shaved his legs, which weren't all that hairy to begin with. But you can see the definition of the muscles better. I like some muscle, on women.

This time he notices *me* looking at *him*. "Back to pamper the drinkers," he says, flicking up his eyebrows as he turns to leave the kitchen.

"Keep 'em happy," I say.

"That's the plan. We want them to come in frequently."

"I would think you'd want them to come here often."

He gives me a confused look. "That's what I said."

"What you said is that you want them to come *in*frequently."

He looks even more confused.

"Forget it," I say. It wasn't much of a joke anyway.

So I'm staring out the window at the street a while later, done for the night but just taking a moment to relax. There are still some loud people at the bar—I can always single out Jack's voice from the rest—and I can feel the vibrations from the piano overhead.

Hector rushes in, untying his apron. "That's it," he says. "Kyle can finish up."

I yawn in reply.

"Still nice out, Danny?" he asks.

"Looks like it."

He takes a blue tube of something from his pocket, shakes out a few drops, and rubs it on his face. "You need some?"

"What is it?"

"Moisturizer."

"I'm plenty moist from washing dishes."

He motions with his hand and heads for the back door. "Come on. Moonrise is at one twenty-two. That's in eleven minutes."

"How do you know that?"

"I just do. . . . They list it in the paper with the tides and all."

So I follow him out. He's walking very quickly, then stops for a second to fix the strap on his sandal. "Hurry. You don't want to miss this," he says as he starts hustling along the sidewalk, not quite running.

The town is quiet—a few people are sitting on decks outside their motel rooms; the lights are still on in the Gypsy Sweethearts dining room. We cut across the Sparhawk lawn and onto the Marginal Way. There's a cool breeze and a lot of stars.

We make the turns and climb the hill and reach the bench above the second of the little coves. Hector checks his watch. "One nineteen."

He stretches out his legs and puts his right elbow on the back of the bench—the elbow closer to me. He's looking out at the ocean.

The water's fairly calm, but I can see the spray where it breaks against the rocks, and it fills the air with the smell of the sea.

I watch the lights of two boats about halfway to the horizon. And gradually I become aware of a glow straight out where the water and the sky meet. At first I think it's another boat coming toward us. But Hector points and whispers, "See?"

"What is it?"

"That's the moon."

The glow gets bigger and brighter, and the moon seems to

emerge from the ocean, throwing its light the length of the water from the horizon to the rocks. Within minutes the entire moon is visible, just above the line, looking huge and full and orangey, already doubling the light around us.

"Something to see, isn't it?" Hector says quietly.

"Awesome. I've never seen that before."

"I saw it happen one night last summer and I couldn't believe how inspiring it was. I never even thought about it before; in Newark, the moon was just up there in the sky most nights. But to see it rising out of the ocean . . ."

Hector's breath is minty, from gum perhaps, or probably a lozenge. I haven't noticed him chewing. He sighs and keeps staring at the moon. He hasn't moved closer to me or anything, but I'm wary. Don't want him to get lost in the moment; before I know it, he'd be grabbing my hand.

"It's really romantic." His voice is soft. "I mean, if you're with the right person."

I don't know if his "right person" is me. I hope not, because if he reaches for me he's gonna get punched. He did say something that intrigues me, though.

"You're from Newark?"

"Yeah."

"I'm from North Jersey, too. Bergenfield."

"I know. That isn't easy to hide."

"Waddayou tawkin' about?" I say.

He laughs.

"So what are you doing in Ogunquit, really?" I ask. "Why here?"

"The lifestyle, obviously. I mean, I went to *Province*town last summer. For about two days. Then I came here. This is less . . . in your face, I suppose."

I nod, though I've never been to Provincetown. I know it's a mostly gay town out on the tip of Cape Cod.

"This is a fantastic place for the summer," he says. "You can be who you are. *Really* be who you are. I don't just mean gay. I'm always gay. Some places force you to be—I don't even know how to describe it—flamboyant or something. *To*tally promiscuous. I got over that my freshman year at Rutgers."

The moon is already a fist's width above the water, and it'll take most of the night for it to reach the other side of the sky. I realize that I'm still sitting sort of tensely, so I lean back on the bench and relax my shoulders.

Hector clears his throat. "Can I tell you about my grandfather?" he asks softly.

"Sure."

"He was an electrician. A one-man company." His voice is just above a whisper. "Avo did jobs in Newark—the Ironbound section; that's the Portuguese area, where we're from—and Harrison and Kearny. Two summers ago I worked with him, just carrying his tools and patching drywall after he'd installed an outlet or helping him snake electrical cables through the walls. After work we'd drink bottles of Miller in his van and he'd tell me things you don't associate with your grandfather when you're a little kid."

Hector is slumped against the back of the bench, his chin pointing almost straight up, his eyes closed. I can hear little birds—sandpipers, I think. There are no lights along the Marginal Way, just whatever comes naturally from the moon and the stars.

A distant rumble of thunder makes him open his eyes. He smiles. "Every day they say 'a forty percent chance of thunderstorms overnight,' but it almost never happens. Just some heat lightning. . . . So he'd tell me about being a teenager in Newark in the fifties, with his parents hardly even speaking English, and how he met my grandmother at some dance and had to fight a guy over her." He laughs gently. "They had four kids and fifteen grandchildren. . . . He died a year ago today. Heart attack."

"Sorry."

"Avo never knew . . . about me. But I think he would have been all right with it."

"You can't tell how people will react, huh?"

"No. . . . Well, with some people you can." He shuts his eyes and slowly shakes his head. "My father . . ."

"Not good?"

"He threatened to kill me. Can you believe that? I mean, he wasn't serious—I don't *think*—but you find out how conditional people's 'love' is when you come out, I can tell you."

I close my eyes now, stretching my legs and digging my heels into the pebbly ground. I don't think my father's feelings for me are necessarily "conditional." He certainly wouldn't want to exterminate me.

Hector might be able to provide some insight on the guy, since they worked together all last summer. He's seen more of him in the past two years than I have. So I ask him, "What's with Jack?"

"Jack . . . He's funny. But I don't know him very well."

"Not real mature, is he?"

"Why should he be? He's a *bar*tender, not a sage."

True. But he *is* a parent. In theory, at least. "You ever see him outside the bar?" I ask.

"Sometimes, out on the street or whatever. He's always running."

"He doesn't run."

"I don't mean like *you* do. He's just always in motion. But I never hang out with him on a night off or anything. I don't think he *takes* any nights off."

"Does everybody, like, sleep around a lot?"

"From the bar?"

"Yeah."

"A lot of people do. Not everybody. *I* don't. . . . I mean I *do*, but not a lot." Hector looks at the fingernails of his right hand for a second. "I've never seen Jack leave with anybody."

"If he did, would he leave with a guy or a woman?"

He laughs. "I'm pretty sure it wouldn't be a guy. Fitch almost never hires straight people, but I don't know about Jack. Why? You interested?"

"No way in hell!" I blush and shake my head hard.

Hector puts his elbow up on the back of the bench again and leans toward me slightly, all playful now. "Who *would* you leave with, given the chance?"

"Me?"

"Yeah *you*. Your dream hookup."

"I hardly know anybody yet."

"So based on what you *do* know." He lifts his eyebrows. "Based on what you can see."

I shift away from him a few inches. "I'm selective, too," I tell him. "So nobody, okay?"

"Fair enough," he says. He looks out at the ocean and I can tell that he's amused. Everybody enjoys a bit of a chase, I suppose.

We walk back a while later. I don't wear a watch, but it has to be way after two. I'm tired as hell. And hungry. Wonder if Jack'll be home. Not likely.

"Why doesn't he hire straight people?" I ask.

"Fitch? He does. Just not very many. It's a gay bar, if you haven't noticed."

"Believe me, I noticed." We've reached the walkway to the house. "I'm back here," I say. "See you tomorrow."

"Pleasant dreams." He stretches that out, sort of teasing: "dreee-ms."

He seems kind and harmless. I enjoyed seeing the moonrise.

But I have to wonder if he's setting me up for something.

Something I could never provide.

# 4

## "Do they have to be male?"

So I go to the Haddock Shack for lunch the next day, showering after my run and walking down Shore Road. The place is small—there's a dozen booths in a horseshoe shape, all with views of the cove, and the kitchen juts out into the middle. All of the booths are full, but some people are finishing up and paying the waitress—not the one I spoke to yesterday—so their booth should open up any second.

I don't like taking a full booth by myself, but there isn't any alternative. The waitress sees me waiting and smiles and waves me over as the other people get up. "I'll just wipe this down," she says, stacking plates and chowder bowls on her arm.

"Busy, huh?" I say as I take a seat.

"Always," she says. "You need a menu?"

"Yeah." I know I want a lobster roll, but I'll see what else they've got.

My target waitress comes out of the kitchen with a big tray of sandwiches and fries and walks to the farthest booth from me. I watch her work, but she doesn't look my way. She goes back to the kitchen and returns with a tray of drinks and chowder for another table.

The tablecloths are red-and-white checked and the walls are knotty pine with framed photos of the cove and mounted cod and lobsters.

The one who seated me has a name tag that says GAIL, which seems appropriate in a town where you get big winds coming off the sea and changing the weather so abruptly. I order my food and hope I can read the other one's name tag from across the room.

I'm halfway done with my meal when she comes over and says, "Hey." Her tag says MERCY. Same ponytail as yesterday; mischievous smile.

"Thought I'd check this place out," I say.

"Like it?"

"Definitely." I gesture with the last of my lobster roll. "This is good."

She tilts her head to one side and I catch a glimpse of a nice little shoulder muscle. "You up here on vacation?" she asks.

"No. I'm living here. At least for the summer. I'm working at Dishes."

"The gay place," she says. A statement, not a question.

"Yeah. . . . Not all of us."

She blushes. "I didn't mean—"

"No problem."

"Looks like a fun place anyway."

"You old enough to go?" I ask.

"Not quite."

"Me either. I just work in the kitchen."

She lifts her eyebrows. "Exciting job. You wash dishes at Dishes."

"I don't mind. It goes fast. The place is always busy."

"Here, too . . . in summer anyway. This town empties out real fast come October." She looks over her shoulder toward her booths. An older lady is trying to flag her down. "Enjoy your meal," she says in a hurry, and walks away.

So I still know virtually nothing about her, but I do like the packaging. I try to catch her eye as I'm leaving, but both waitresses are hustling their butts off trying to keep up, looking slightly frazzled and athletic. There are at least a dozen people waiting for seats as I exit.

"Hey, wait!" she calls from the doorway.

I'm about fifteen feet away. I take one step toward her and tilt my head in expectation. She walks about halfway to me with a challenging smile. "Did you have your nap yesterday?"

I blush. "No . . . I just daydreamed."

She shrugs and puffs out her lips. "I did a little of that, too." Then she turns and goes back inside.

The cove is swarming with tourists. I walk the short paved loop around the perimeter and look in the windows of the trinket and T-shirt shops. The galleries are full of seascapes and Marginal Way images.

There's a strong fishy smell by the dock where the lobster boats come in, but it isn't unpleasant at all. Dozens of boats are anchored in the cove: *Bittersweet, Deborah Ann, Finestkind.* Little dories and rowboats are tied to the dock.

So she was daydreaming about *me*? Seemed like she was saying so. Worth pursuing, for sure.

The ocean looks different today from yesterday, which was different from the day before that. Today it's as flat as a lake and a shiny metallic blue. I head for the Marginal Way. It leads uphill out of the cove, following the uneven shoreline until you're thirty feet above the water. Then it winds back down and keeps climbing and descending and twisting.

I stop and inhale the salty aroma from the sea crashing on the rocks. Then I climb down, closer to the ocean, scouting for places where two bodies might fit comfortably without stones jabbing into our butts.

I've never had a girlfriend. Sex I've had, but it's not that hard to come by in college. Not when you live in a dorm that has keg parties three nights a week.

Okay, it *is* hard to come by. At least for me. But I pulled it off twice and I wasn't a jerk about it. Might be nice to have a bond that would last more than twenty minutes, though. Maybe even a whole summer.

On the walk back to town, I have to go slow to avoid colliding with all the people. But I'm in no hurry. It's only frustrating on mornings when I run the path, constantly saying "Pardon" (with a long *O*—a lot of these people are from Quebec).

The lifeguards at the Little Beach, halfway along the path,

seem to be paying more attention to each other than the bathers. A guy and a girl, maybe eighteen or nineteen, with good tans. The girl is wearing sunglasses and has great legs. She's eating an apple and laughing at something the guy is saying. He must be one of those guys who knows what to say to girls.

A lady with white hair and a big sun hat has her easel set up next to one of the benches. She smiles at me as I walk past.

"Mind if I look?" I ask.

"Not at all."

The painting shows a long curve in the rocks, and you can see the flat, whiter sands of Wells Beach way in the distance. But the focal point of the painting is the gray-shingled house high above us, with its dark-green trellises and widow's walk.

"Your place?" I ask.

"Don't I wish," she says. "That's a two-million-dollar property if it's a dime." She takes a closer look at me. "Vacationing?"

"Not really. You?"

"No. I've been here forever. I come down here every day."

"All winter, too?"

"Never miss a day." She waves her hand toward the water. "That's my life force. Can't you feel it?"

"Yeah. I do."

"It's different every day, but it never really changes. . . . I'll never leave this place." She sets down the paintbrush. "I expect to be here forever. I mean that. *Forever.*"

On the way back, I walk past four guys about my age coming toward me. Last summer I rented a house at the Jersey Shore for six weeks with nine other guys. I was working at a deli in Bergenfield, but I got down there a couple of nights a week. We never slept—just drank and played poker and lived like pigs. They're down there again this summer. I chose this instead.

I was beginning to think I'd made the wrong choice and was destined for a long and lonely summer.

But maybe the universe is about to show me some Mercy.


The two former UMass softball players are at the bar drinking beer and joking around with Jack. I bring out a tray of glasses so I can say hello. They stare at me like I'm vaguely familiar.

"I bumped into you on the Marginal Way the other night," I say.

"Oh, yeah," says the bigger one. "The runner."

"You here all summer?" I ask.

"Two weeks. You?"

I look at Jack and say, "Undetermined."

"Great atmosphere for you," says the smaller one. "Young guy, good looking . . . You're in the right place."

Yeah, if you like men. I just shrug. "Not a lot of action back in the kitchen."

Jack picks up the bigger one's empty glass and starts to refill it with beer. Then he points toward the kitchen with this thumb. "Back to the galley," he says. So I go.

Hector comes into the kitchen a while later through the swinging door and says hi, then leans against the prep table and watches me scrub a frying pan. It's early yet; the mob scene starts soon.

"So, do you like sports?" he asks out of nowhere.

"Some of them."

"Me, too."

"Yeah?" I ask. "Like what?"

"I played baseball in high school. Well, I didn't exactly *play* much. I was a relief pitcher."

This surprises me. Hector doesn't seem very athletic; even though he's thin, he looks kind of soft under the shoulder blades, as if he used to be chubby and still carries some of the remnants.

"You like baseball?" he asks.

"Somewhat. I like individual sports more, like track."

"Oh. I went out for wrestling when I was a freshman," he says. "I was a fat little boy and I got absolutely crushed. . . . But it was exciting, too."

"In what way?" I say this somewhat pointedly to suggest that there's a distinction between athletic excitement and glandular arousal.

He gets what I mean and flicks up his eyebrows. "On many levels," he says with a smile.

What am I doing? I'm flirting with this guy? Better change the tone.

"I like boxing," I say. That ought to scare him off.

"Doing it or watching?"

"Watching."

He raises his fists and throws out a few jabs. "Brutal game," he says.

So what am I supposed to say when he asks me out? I can feel that coming in the playful way he's talking. That ain't happening, but I don't want to hurt him, either.

He looks at his fingernails and starts scraping at one edge with his thumbnail. "Are you doing anything on Tuesday?"

I wince a little. "I don't know," I say. "What's up?"

The place is closed on Tuesdays; he knows I'm probably available. (That will actually be the last day we're closed until after Labor Day; we'll go seven days a week starting July 1.)

He spreads the fingers of his hand and closes them into a fist. "I was wondering . . ."

Here it comes.

He clears his throat. "Do you play softball?"

"Huh?"

"There's that Lobsterfest Tournament. Fitch said if I could find ten players, he'd sponsor us. You'd make eight."

"Um, yeah. I don't think I have a glove with me, but I could scrounge one up."

His face brightens. "Good. Now we just need two more."

"Do they have to be male?"

"No. Not at all."

"Give me a minute. I got the perfect solution."

I head back toward the bar to talk to the lesbians.

"Watch that door," he says.

I stop with my hand against the door that leads out of the kitchen and give him a questioning look.

Hector is blushing lightly and grinning. "That one swings both ways," he says.

* * *

Several new people started tonight; they've got four bartenders at the long bar upstairs, plus an extra dishwasher down here, I'm happy to say. The pace has been frantic for the past three hours and I'd never keep up by myself. Capacity upstairs is supposed to be 120 people, but there's got to be at least 200. And there are four new waiters I've never seen before.

Hector is on his third T-shirt of the night; he sprays on cologne with each change, too. He and one of the newly arrived waiters—Chase, who's apparently putting in his second summer here—were giving each other shoulder rubs in the kitchen a few minutes ago.

Everybody seems elated to have Chase back. I've seen him kiss three different guys on the lips already. He's the type who loves to primp in front of the giant mirror between the bathrooms.

Jack sends me upstairs with a case of Saratoga water, so I go through the downstairs bar room and up to the piano lounge. Sal the marshmallow bouncer is at the top of the stairs singing along: "Clang, clang, clang went the trolley. . . ." He gives me a friendly nod. I guess he's about twenty-five—geeky haircut, Hawaiian shirt, dress shoes. Can't imagine him being much of a bouncer. I mean, *he'd* bounce plenty, but he's way too shy to confront anyone.

One of the new bartenders wipes his brow with his hand and takes the case of blue bottles from me, then goes back to mixing martinis.

Downstairs, I finish scrubbing a pan and leave some others

soaking in the sink. I need some air and a change of scenery, if only for a couple of minutes.

It's after eleven, but the sidewalk is busy with people walking; even little kids are still out with their parents. I cross the street and take a seat on one of the benches in front of Fancy That. I'd estimate that thirty people walk by every minute, including at least one girl that I follow as far as I can with my eyes. I'm watching one when I feel a poke on my shoulder.

"Hi," I say, surprised to see Mercy, the waitress from Perkins Cove.

"You have the night off?" she asks. She's wearing a brown hooded sweatshirt that says ADDISON COLLEGE.

I shake my head. "I'm on a break. They brought in another dishwasher, so I can take a few minutes."

"A local guy?"

"No. He's Russian or something. Sergei."

"Sir *Gay*?"

"Right."

"The young Bulgarian guys are the best foreign workers," she says. A lot of the summer help around here are Eastern Europeans on some sort of exchange program; the rest are either local New Englanders or Caribbean.

She brushes a strand of hair back under her hood. "The thing is, they've always got that dark, brush-cutty hair and an ugly mole or something on their cheek or their forehead. I went out with one of them from work last week, but . . . too homely."

"Where'd you go?"

"The movies."

"This one?"

"Yeah."

The creaky old movie theater across the street has six hundred seats but just one screen and only opens in the summer. They get decent films. The highlight of the year, apparently, is the *Sound of Music* sing-along weekend in August, when everyone gets a lyric sheet on the way in and stands and sings with every number.

A trolley goes by. This one is Rolly, which you don't see as often as the others. I think there are eight of them: Lolly, Holly, Dolly, Polly, Wally, Jolly, and Molly are the others. They run around town all day and till after midnight for a buck.

"So what are you up to?" I ask.

"Just felt like eating some junk." She holds up a crusty pastry thing she must have got at the Village Food Market. "And to see if anybody interesting was around."

"Don't let me stop you." I stand. "I'll go with you."

"Okay. You want a bite of this?"

"Sure." The pastry is kind of bland, surprisingly. "You go to Addison?"

"I'll be a junior."

It's a liberal-arts school in Boston. I don't know anything else about it. But I ask the usual "What's your major?" thing.

"Art. Minor in French."

"You paint or what?"

"Mostly paint. It's my passion. Are you in school?"

"Yeah. I think so."

She rolls her eyes. "You're not sure?"

"I'll probably be up here this fall. I dropped out after last semester."

We reach the end of the business area and she stops. "Do you have to get right back?"

I shrug. "In a bit. The quicker I get back the quicker I get out."

We walk past the stores again—only the VFM and Fancy That are still open; you can get ice-cream cones at either place.

"Interesting in what way?" I finally ask.

She shrugs and gives me a smirk. "Well, I've always found dishwashers to be particularly fascinating."

We've reached the side of the Front Porch, the town's other piano bar. A hundred voices upstairs are singing "One Singular Sensation."

I joke around, saying, "Thanks for a wonderful evening."

She half smiles. "We'll have to do it again sometime."

"Right . . . so, what do you paint? Seascapes?"

She lets out a huffy snort. "When I was *eleven*."

"Oh."

"My stuff is less representational than that. It's hard to describe."

"I'll have to see for myself."

"I was always an art nerd," she says, leaning against the brick building and putting both hands in her sweatshirt pouch. Her jeans are stretched tight across her strong-looking thighs and there's a sizable rip above one knee. "That and soccer and marching band. I never even went on a date until I got to college."

"Was it worth the wait?"

She laughs. "It put me a few years behind. . . . Anyway, what's *your* passion?"

I shake my head slowly while I think about it. "Track, I guess."

She nods. "You look really fit." She says this as if she thinks that's a good thing.

"I mean, I'm kind of directionless right now. As far as track. But as soon as I get back in school . . ."

She raises her eyebrows. "You sure don't need to be in school to run."

"Or to paint. It kind of helps give it some definition, but yeah, I run just as hard whether I'm on a team or not."

So what am I supposed to say to ask her out? She can probably feel it coming, and she's looking at me sort of hopefully, I think. So I just ask. "You get any days off?"

"A few. Tuesday this week."

"Me, too. Probably be my last night off for a while."

"So . . ." Her eyes narrow. "What was your name?"

"Dan . . . Danny."

"Okay, Dan-Danny. Meet you somewhere Tuesday night?"

"How about right here? Nine o'clock."

"I'll be here," she says.

"Me, too."

As soon as I see Hector, I realize that I've now got two things scheduled for Tuesday.

"It'll be over by eight thirty at the absolute latest," he says. "There aren't any lights at the field."

"Great."

"We'll probably all get together and go out somewhere after."

Probably someplace I can't get into, but I won't be joining them anyway. He's hoping, I assume, that I'll tag along with them and we'll end up alone on the Marginal Way again. I don't think so. Go out there a second time and I'd really be asking for it.

He reaches over and gently wipes some pastry crumbs from the corner of my mouth. "So what position do you like?"

He sees my confusion and adds, "In softball?"

I wipe a disturbing image from my mind and answer, "Anywhere. I haven't played in a while, so maybe the outfield."

"Chase gets center field," he says. "He's *incredibly* athletic."

"Then I'll play left."

"I'll put you in right. More people hit it there."

It's hard not to notice Chase's muscularity, the long, lean calves. He's got short blondish hair and glasses, with a tattoo of an eagle on his left bicep. All of the waiters seem to wear leather flip-flops.

"I'm so glad he's back," Hector says. "You'll see. He's a ton of fun. And *so* sexy."

# 5

# "There wasn't anything much to feel."

So I hit two doubles and Hector pitched great as we won our game over the Ogunquit Arts Alliance. Had to get up sadistically early for the eight a.m. start (we had the first of the four opening-round games), but we all stumbled to the field on time and did good.

Anna, the larger of the UMass pair, flexed her muscles and hit a mammoth three-run homer in the first inning and we cruised from there. I think the final score was 14–2.

This afternoon ought to be a different story. We've got the fire department in the semifinals. I eat lunch at home and walk back to the field. Most of the team is already there, tossing a ball around or stretching in right field.

The Robert Perkins Memorial Field (people have the balls to refer to it as "the stadium") is a flat, somewhat grassy area on the wooded side of Route 1, about a quarter mile from the downtown area. It has a low chain-link fence around the outfield and a high backstop, and there are six rows of aluminum bleachers stretching for maybe twenty yards along the third-base line. No dugouts, just wooden benches behind short, freestanding lengths of fence. There are rectangular sponsor signs lining the outfield fence with names like Maxwell Realty, Barnacle Billy's Restaurant, and the Anchorage Inn.

"How's the arm?" I say to Hector as I walk past. It turned out that he has a pretty good whip there, generating some power on his delivery.

"Still feels good," he says. He's wearing a brand-new yellow baseball cap with no logo and his arm smells like mentholated muscle cream. "If we get a big lead, I might bring Jack in to pitch and save my arm for the final."

I do a few strides across the outfield to loosen up, then notice Mercy sitting in the bleachers: orange top, long shorts, blue running shoes. I wave too energetically.

Since she's watching, I do a few more strides before walking over to her. She stands up.

"You're playing?" she asks.

"Yeah."

"For the gay team?" She glances toward our side of the field.

"Mostly. We *won* this morning."

"I'm impressed." Doesn't sound like it.

"You should've seen us."

"Well, I'm here now." She juts her chin toward left field, where the firemen are warming up. They're actually in full uniforms—

white with red trim and red caps with OFD above the brim. We're in the blue waiters' T-shirts and whatever shorts we felt like wearing.

"These guys won the whole tournament last year," Mercy says.

"Did you see it?"

She shrugs. "Part of it. There's not a whole lot else to do on a Tuesday afternoon. And my brother's on the team."

"Which one?"

She points to a short muscular guy with a thick mustache. He's balding on top.

"He a lot older than you?"

"Ten years. He's the oldest of us."

"How many others?"

"Three sisters, then me."

"They all still around here?"

"I've got two sisters up in Portland and one in Boston. Only Buddy still lives here."

"And you."

"Yeah, well, only when I'm home from school."

The home-plate umpire steps onto the field and pulls down his face mask. The firemen jog to their positions.

"See you later," I say, and hustle across the field.

Hector is standing with his arms crossed as I reach the bench. "So who was *that*?" he asks.

"This girl I know."

"Oh." He smiles and rubs his chin. "A *girl*."

"Actually, we're going out later."

"Oooh. Tonight?"

"Tonight."

"Where to?"

"I don't know. We're just meeting in town. I don't know what."

"Where'd you find her?"

"I've just seen her around."

I'm up third, so I grab a bat and step away from Hector, swinging it a few times.

"We can't have these romantic distractions," he says. "Keep your head on the *game*, Danny."

"Sorry, Coach."

Jack, leading off, pops up to second, so I step to the on-deck circle.

"She's *watch*ing," Hector says melodically.

"I'll give her something to watch. I'm going to hit a home run."

"That'll impress her for sure. You batting righty or lefty?"

"I always bat righty."

He sticks the very tip of his tongue between his lips and catches my eye, then looks out at the field. "I'm surprised," he says. "I was sure you were a switch-hitter."

"You wish." I flex my bicep and give him a very manly look.

Chase is at bat with two strikes already. He swings awkwardly at the next pitch, then walks glumly toward our bench. "He's got some heat," he says to me.

Mercy's brother is catching. I give him a quick nod as I step in. The pitcher is tall and lean and looks about forty, with straight greasy hair hanging out of the cap.

I kick at the dirt and pull back the bat and wait for the pitch.

"So, how do you know my sister?" I hear.

I turn slightly and look over my shoulder and start to speak. The ball smacks into the catcher's glove and the umpire calls, "Strike!"

"Nice one," I say.

Mercy's brother laughs, throws the ball back, and punches his glove.

The second pitch is high and outside. I watch it go by and my teammates shout encouragement.

The infield's playing back and I'm feeling quick, so as soon as the pitch is on its way I square to bunt. It's never been my strong suit, but I catch this one perfectly and it rolls down the third-base line. I sprint full speed and feel a twinge in my ankle, but I don't hear the ball hit the first baseman's glove until a split second after I reach the base.

Hector is clapping and the others are yelling. I limp back to the base and rub my ankle. Anna's up. She and her partner, Coral, are the only women in the game.

Jack comes off the bench with a freshly lit cigarette and stands in the coach's box behind first base. "Nice hustle," he says. "Good bunt, too."

"Thanks." He taught me to bunt when I was seven. Also how to shuffle cards, burp the alphabet, and make fart sounds by wetting my armpit and flapping my arm up and down.

I take a small lead, but I won't try to steal. Anna's not a singles hitter.

She whacks the first pitch high and deep and there's no question that it's gone. I circle the bases, waving much more suavely to Mercy this time as I round third, and stop at the plate to wait for Anna.

Buddy's got his catcher's mask off and he's frowning, shaking his head slowly. "At least *she's* manly," I hear him mumble.

We don't get much offense after that. Their pitcher is tough to hit. They've got some power of their own, but Chase and I each make a couple of catches near the fence and we hold our lead for a few innings. They finally get a run in the fourth and tie it up in the fifth. We scratch out one more on Kyle's double, but they get it right back in the sixth and then load the bases with two outs.

Hector is still on the mound, but his pitches are losing speed and he's sweating heavily. The temperature is pushing ninety, but there's a breeze and we've got a tub of ice with water and soda.

Sal the bouncer must be really suffering behind the plate. He has to weigh at least three hundred. To call him a bouncer is stretching it anyway—he checks the IDs and makes sure the stairs are kept clear, but if there's any sign of trouble, Jack and the other bartenders would jump in immediately. Sal is one of the gentlest people I've met.

Anyway, Anna's playing first base and Coral is our shortstop. Jack plays second, Kyle the waiter is at third, and Bernie, an upstairs bartender, is out in left field. The nine of us have played the entire game. Our only subs are Alex—a Russian waiter who's never played softball before—and Diego—a sheet-metal worker from Boston who's a consistent weekend customer. Alex pinch-hit for Kyle this morning and struck out; Diego played two innings in left.

Mercy's brother comes up and drives a long one toward the fence in right-center. Chase and I converge on it and he waves me off, snagging the ball just as it would have cleared the fence.

So we go into the top of the last inning tied.

Sal walks over to a tree behind the bench and slumps to the ground. Hector helps him peel off his shirt, then dips it in the tub of ice water and wrings it over Sal's head. He hands Sal a two-liter bottle of Pepsi, then sends Diego up to pinch-hit for him. Diego is a short wiry guy in his thirties, with dark hair and eyes.

"You'll have to catch, too," Hector calls.

"No problem." Diego lines the first pitch safely up the middle for a single.

Sal leans up on his elbows and says, "Who *is* that guy?"

"Diego," Hector says, looking at Sal like he's a lunatic.

"He can hit!" Sal says. "Why hasn't he been in there all along?"

"Because *you* were."

"Sounds like poor management to me. We may have to schedule an impeachment between games."

Hector reaches over and messes Sal's hair. "That's the thanks I get for playing favorites?"

Jack takes a few ferocious swings and smirks at the pitcher, who seems to be losing some zip. He hits the first pitch along the ground right at the second baseman, but it takes a nasty late hop and hits the guy in the shoulder. Diego slides into second and Jack beats the throw to first.

I feel a nice surge of adrenaline. Two on, no outs.

The firemen are looking frustrated. A few of them have made some comments under their breaths during the game, like the occasional *faggot* or *pussy*.

"Let's do it, Chase," Hector calls.

But for all the hype Hector gave him, Chase hasn't proven to be much of a hitter. He strikes out for the third time in this game, leaving me the task of bringing in the lead run.

I take a pitch that looks outside, but the umpire calls it a strike. Jack raises his fist and nods at me hard. I smack the next one into the hole between first and second. The second baseman lunges and knocks it down, then throws me out. But we've got two runners in scoring position and Anna's coming up.

They know better than to pitch to her, though. Hector's on deck and he hasn't had a hit all day. So Anna takes four outside pitches and jogs to first.

Hector taps the bat against his left shoe, then the right. He frowns at the pitcher and steps in.

The first pitch is at Hector's chin, and he lurches out of the way just in time. Jack calls, "Hey!" in what sounds like a challenge, and the pitcher turns to him and glares. Jack glares back until the guy turns to the plate.

Hector swings and misses at the next one, and the fielders shout encouragement. Mercy's brother pounds his glove.

Hector swings even harder at the next one and gets a piece

of the ball. It bloops over the shortstop and falls to the grass in left. Diego scores easily, and Jack—in typical Jack fashion—comes racing around third toward the plate, head back, teeth clenched, and arms flailing.

But the outfielders were playing in, and the guy in left gets to the ball on the first bounce. He rifles it toward home and Mercy's brother grabs it as Jack barrels into him. They both go flying to the dirt past the plate, but the umpire calls Jack out and the inning is over.

But we've got the lead. We all mob Hector as he comes off the field. Three more outs and we're in the final.

It takes four pitches: a long fly out to Chase, a line drive right back at Hector, a called strike, and a groundout to second.

We walk toward the plate to shake hands, but a few of the firemen just walk away. Mercy's brother shakes my hand but doesn't make eye contact. Their pitcher and Jack are standing toe to toe a few feet away, and I hear "chicken shit" and "ass wipe."

Diego steps between them and grabs Jack's arm, pulling him away. Jack acts like he's resisting but he starts walking. He shakes out of Diego's grasp and punches him lightly on the shoulder. "I'm good," he says. He heads over to see how Sal is doing.

Diego walks next to me, shaking his head. "Those guys can't believe they could lose to us," he says. "Listen. Look at me. I love sports. I work in sheet metal. I'm not 'feminate. . . . I'm gay; I'm not a fag."

He turns and looks across the infield. A couple of the firemen are milling around, looking disgusted.

"We kicked their asses," Diego says.

"Yeah, we did."

I get a bottle of water from the tub and then wipe my face with my icy hand. We've got at least three hours before the final. The players from the Lighthouse and the Realtors Association are warming up for the second semifinal.

Mercy comes by and I ask her if she wants to walk down to Perkins Cove. She nods.

"Nice game," she says.

"You surprised?"

"My brother sure was."

I've wondered what straight guys who grew up here think about the huge influx of gay people every summer. But the town's been like this for so long that I didn't think it'd be a big deal anymore. I mean, at least half the businesses seem to be gay-owned and even some of the selectmen and other "community leaders" are. But Jack says if you mention in neighboring towns that you're from Ogunquit, people sort of look at you and say, "Oh," as if just living here as a single man is akin to coming out.

"I guess he expected a limp-wristed lineup," I say.

"He sure didn't expect to lose. None of them did."

I smile in a self-satisfied way. "Pretty humbling, I guess."

"They'll go cry in their beers," she says with a laugh. "They'll get over it. . . . How's your ankle?"

"It's okay. I just tweaked it a little. I'm impressed that you noticed."

"You were limping."

"Not much."

We walk down Shore Road past the churches and the gravel

parking lot and The Impastable Dream, then turn off into the cove past more restaurants and shops and bed-and-breakfast inns.

"I'm thirsty as hell," I say. "You want anything?"

"Yeah. Let's hit the candy shop."

I get a soda and she scoops some chocolate-covered almonds out of a bin into a white paper bag. She points to the ice-cream shop and tells me she had her first job there. Then we sit on a bench between the drawbridge and Barnacle Billy's, the biggest restaurant down here.

She points at a large red boat, the *Ugly Anne*, which is slowly pulling out of the cove. "*Ugly Ass*," she says, giggling. "I used to come down here with my sister Faith and we'd make up funny names for all the boats."

"Faith and Mercy. What are your other sisters' names?"

"Hope and Joy."

"Wow."

"My parents are hopelessly Christian."

"Faith is closest to you? In age?"

"Yeah. She just graduated from Boston College. We have this apartment—an absolute hole on Commonwealth Avenue, but it has three bedrooms—with four other girls. She's still down there looking for a job."

Mercy points at another boat, a smaller white one with *Marcia Beal* on the hull. "That's the *Munchy Meal*," she says. "There's the *Queen of Piss*. . . . You try one."

I'm looking at the *Lizzy B* and searching my head for a lesbian reference, but nothing is gelling.

"*Happy Whore*," she says, pointing to the *Happy Hour*.

I finally come up with *Titline* for the party boat *Tautline*. It makes her laugh.

"Pretty wild game for a bunch of Christians," I say.

"You should have heard us in Sunday school."

"Never been."

"You didn't miss much." She tosses the empty candy bag into a trash bin marked BENEVOLENCE and motions with her hand that we ought to keep walking. We head across to the Marginal Way.

She busts my chops like a guy would and doesn't seem to mind getting it back. I've lost some potential girlfriends by going too far with the wittiness; they usually decided I was a jerk. They were probably right.

She's confident enough to make fun of me, but that confidence wavers enough to be appealing. There's a shyness there, too. I like her attitude. And her athletic body. Maybe I already mentioned that.

"So you played soccer, huh?" I ask. "Any other sports?"

"Well . . . I wrestled some. My freshman year."

Where have I heard that before? "What made you do that?"

"Buddy had been really good at it, and I went to all of his matches when I was little. So I went out; I mean, it wasn't *that* unusual. People make a big deal about it, but girls do wrestle sometimes." She turns her head and looks over the water toward the horizon. Today the ocean is tea-green and choppy. The tide is in. "I wrestled jayvee. I was scrawny, so . . ."

"The other guys weren't feeling you up during the matches?"

She rolls her eyes and frowns. "There wasn't anything much

to feel. I weighed ninety-one pounds, which was small for even the lightest weight class, but I went four-and-four that season. I didn't like the pressure, so I didn't go back out as a sophomore."

"And you weren't so scrawny anymore?"

"Not everywhere."

A little boy about three and a girl about five come scurrying along the path, twenty yards ahead of their parents. The boy is carrying a pinecone. He looks up and says, *"Bonjour,"* as we pass.

We nod to the parents—the mom is pushing an empty stroller and the guy has a small backpack.

"Those kids must be very bright to be able to speak French at such a young age," I say.

"Funny."

My ankle hurts slightly—not enough to be a big deal, but it would probably do it some good to soak it in that cold water. So I start making my way down the rocks and she follows.

There's a smooth slope above the edge of a tide pool, and the water is rushing in and out so it won't be warmed up. I take off my shoes and socks and start very carefully down the slope.

My caution is useless, because the wet rock is incredibly slippery and my feet fly out from under me. My left shin scrapes the rock as I go down, and I flail with my hands to brace myself. I hit directly on my face, just under my eye, and keep sliding until my feet are in the water.

Mercy starts toward me, but I say, "Stop! It's slippery as hell."

"I've got my shoes on," she says, scuttling down the rock. She grabs my hand and says, "You all right?"

I laugh, embarrassed. My cheek is stinging, but I feel my jaw and check my teeth and everything seems intact. "Just stupid," I say. "It's like frickin' greased or something. I had nothing to grip."

"You're bleeding."

I touch the sore spot. It's swelling, but the blood flow is minimal. I wipe it with salt water and climb onto the rock, keeping hold of her hand and not getting off my knees until I reach a dry spot.

"You get no traction with those bare feet," she says.

"No kidding."

We sit there for a few minutes, looking out at the surf.

"You sure it's okay?" she asks. "We could go to my house and get a Band-Aid and some cream."

"I'll be all right."

She takes out some Kleenex and dabs at it.

"Still bleeding?" I ask.

"No. It's oozing some clear stuff, but it looks pretty clean."

"Good. Let's go."

I read more people's T-shirts as we walk: STONEHILL HOCKEY; BUCKNELL INTRAMURALS; SHIPPENSBURG TRACK AND FIELD. We get to the tiny lighthouse by the only road that reaches all the way to the Marginal Way. It leads up into Israel Head and all the old sea captains' mansions.

"You been up here?" she asks.

"I ran through a few times."

"There's a cool cemetery. You ever seen it?"

"No."

So we walk up a very steep hill, then start down the other side. The streets of Israel Head have no sidewalks and the properties are heavy with huge maples and pines. In coastal Maine you can live in the forested mountains and be only a few feet from the ocean.

The cemetery is on a grassy slope and has a low, spiky iron fence.

"We've got a lot of family in here," Mercy says. "From way back."

I see stones from the early- and mid-1800s; most of them are marked LITTLEFIELD or PERKINS or MAXWELL.

"This is us," she says as we reach a section of fairly simple white stones and a few small monuments.

The earliest one I see is Winfield Hartwell, 1832. There's Captain Elias Hartwell and Captain Josiah; Reverend Benjamin and Reverend Aaron; Constance, Lucinda, Jeremiah, and dozens of others.

"Four families really dominate the town history," she says. "We're one of 'em."

I nod. My family roots are basically dust. "What does your family do now?" I ask.

"On the Hartwell side? My dad teaches at the high school in Wells. My mom—she's a Maxwell—she runs the library. My uncle owns a lobster boat. My brother does dock work down in Portsmouth."

She kneels and straightens a Memorial Day wreath on one of the gravestones. "There's still some gentility in the family. Not us, though."

"You want to keep living here?"

She shrugs and we start walking down the hill, back toward Shore Road. "Not right away. But I'll be back sometime. . . . It's home.

"So," she says, "is everybody on the team gay except two of you?"

"Which two? I mean, which other one?"

"The guy who collided with my brother in the last inning? He isn't, right?"

"Jack. Right. You know him?"

"Not really."

"I *think* everybody else is."

"The fat guy?"

"Sal? I assume so. He likes Judy Garland songs."

She smiles. "Well, that clinches it."

"He *seems* gay. You know, sweet and kind and sensitive."

"They aren't *all* that way, you know."

"Well, he is."

"Yeah, well a lot of them are assholes, just like anybody else."

We turn the corner back toward town and walk past the Presbyterian church and a French restaurant. "What's Buddy's real name?" I ask.

"Osborne."

"*Osborne?*"

"Yeah. It's been in our family forever. . . . Hey, you never said anything about *your* family."

"Not much to say. My mom works at a Wal-Mart in New

Jersey; she never got married. My dad kind of left her to fend for herself. I think she's slept in the same bedroom every night of her life. We lived with my grandparents."

"So your dad wasn't around?"

I hesitate. "You know the guy who crashed into your brother?"

"*That's* your father?" She seems startled.

"Yeah . . . more like a roommate than a dad."

"Oh . . . 'kay."

"You *do* know him?"

"I've seen him around."

"But you don't know him?"

"He . . . hit on me once. Like, two years ago."

"Get out! Where?"

"On the beach."

"Get out! My father?"

"Yeah. It was him. I'm sure he doesn't remember."

"But you do."

"Of course. It was memorable. He's, like, twice my age."

"Was he a jerk about it?"

"No. He was just flirting. It only lasted two minutes. It wasn't like we were alone. The beach was packed. He was just, like, 'Nice day. Nice breeze. Nice ass.'"

"What'd *you* do?"

"Well, the 'nice ass' comment wasn't right away. I was talking to him, you know, like a teenager to an adult. About *surfing*, I think. *I* wasn't flirting, believe me. It came out of nowhere."

"Guess he figured you were worth a try."

"I'm half his age."

We walk a block or two in silence while I think this over. Then I speak. "He was right, by the way. You know . . . about your butt."

She ignores the comment. Doesn't respond anyway. But I'm perceptive; I feel the sudden ice. She's thinking that I'm just as much of a jerk as he is.

I put it another way. "He has good taste."

"Shitty judgment, though."

"I guess so."

That's been in *our* family forever.

# 6

## "Just give me half a minute with some gel."

Jack is staring at us as we reach the field. Mercy climbs into the bleachers and I go over to him. He reaches toward my face. "That from the game?"

I pull back so he can't touch it. "No. It just happened."

He breaks into a grin. "You put your hands in the wrong place?"

"What do you mean?"

"She let you have it?"

"Who?"

"That girl you walked off with."

I laugh. "Get outta here."

"So what the hell'd you do?"

"Fell on the rocks down by the ocean."

"Good move. So who is she?"

"You don't recognize her?"

"Why would I?"

Yeah, why would he? He's probably hit on a thousand women since then. "Her name's Mercy. I don't know, she works down at the Haddock Shack."

"Looks fairly hot. . . . I was starting to wonder."

"About what?"

"About how you've been buddying up with Hector."

I shrug. "Don't wonder."

"I *wasn't*. But nice to see some contradictory evidence."

"You mean her?"

"Yeah."

"We're going out later."

"That's my boy. We know how to pick 'em."

"At least I *think* we still are."

"You think?"

"Not sure."

"Because she belted you?" He laughs.

"She did *not* belt me."

He bends down and picks up a clod of dirt and rubs it into his hands. "They all wind up wanting to belt us sooner or later," he says. "We're men, right? We screw up and say stupid shit. Can't help it. It's how we're programmed."

Hector claps his hands three times. "All right, team. Let's do it." We all gather around him. "This is the first time two gay bars have ever made it to the championship round."

"Historical moment," Chase says.

"Historical or hysterical?" Jack asks.

"Both!" Hector says. "Now let's pound their asses. Show them who's boss."

We're up first again. Hector's shifted our lineup slightly. Diego is catching. Coral is batting second, and Chase—who can't hit worth a shit—moves down to sixth, behind Hector.

I stand next to Hector near the bench. He notices my face and his mouth falls open. "God, that looks sore."

"It's not so bad. Don't touch it."

"I wouldn't. But you ought to put some ointment on it."

"It'll be all right."

"Eeesh," he says. "She's got claws, huh?"

I just roll my eyes. "I fell on a rock."

The Lighthouse players take the field, and Hector scans their lineup. "They have the *worst* help over there," he says.

"Oh, yeah?"

"You wouldn't *believe*. All the best waiters are at our place or the Front Porch."

The pitcher takes a few warm-up tosses while Jack eyes him from the on-deck circle.

"This guy any good?" I ask Hector. The pitcher is tall and lanky and well-coifed, with a hundred-dollar haircut and sporty sunglasses.

Hector applies some lip balm and stares at my injured face again. "I have no idea if he can pitch, but he's a *horrible* waiter. He worked at our place for a few weeks last summer. *So* lazy, but he's very good at it. Being lazy, I mean. He can carry a napkin around for two hours and make it look like he's doing something essential to the operation. I think he's the only person Fitch ever got worked up enough about to fire."

Jack strikes out. So does Coral, who's been a consistent hitter all day. The Lighthouse pitcher isn't particularly fast, but his ball moves oddly and dips sharply when it reaches the plate.

He strikes me out, too.

They make a lot of noise coming off the field. We take our positions stoically. Sal the bouncer stands up by the bench and shouts, "Dishes pride!" We all clap. With mitts on, it sounds flat and muffled.

We come to bat in the seventh inning (scheduled to be the last) tied 4–4. These have been the highlights:

- Anna led off the second with her third home run of the day on the first pitch of the inning. The thing went *way* beyond the fence. The Lighthouse pitcher switched primarily to fastballs after that, and we managed to get some hits.

- Chase walked in the fourth inning, flirted with the blond (dyed) first baseman for a couple of pitches, then got picked off while leaning toward him to whisper something.

- Jack hit a clean double into the left-center gap in the fifth, was about to be out by a mile trying to stretch it into a triple—until the third baseman with the shaved head muffed the catch—then managed to score with a vicious slide that knocked the double-earringed catcher onto his back. That gave us our first lead of the game. They tied it up in the bottom of the inning.

· I struck out for the second time to end the fifth. I'd grounded out in the third.

Diego's leading off the seventh, then we've got the top of the order. It's nearly seven thirty, so the air is slightly cooler now and the sun is on the downswing. I sit next to Sal and say, "This is it."

"The tough get going," he says. He's got his arms folded across his flabby chest. He shouts, "Di-e-GO!"

We pick up the chant. "Di-e-GO! Di-e-GO!"

He bows toward us and grins.

The Lighthouse pitcher is looking fatigued, letting out an audible grunt with each windmill pitch. He runs the count to 3-and-2, and then Diego fouls off a couple of more.

The catcher calls time and jogs to the mound. They both look at the first baseman, then wave him over to talk. They all go back to their positions and Diego takes ball four.

We erupt in cheers. All we need is one run and some defense and the gleaming trophy will be ours. (It's about two feet tall with a molded gold lobster on top, spreading its claws. The plate says OGUNQUIT LOBSTERFEST SOFTBALL TOURNAMENT CHAMPIONS. Jack's already cleared a place for it between some liquor bottles behind the bar. For now, it's sitting on a table by the backstop.)

Jack comes up, lays down a sacrifice bunt, and moves Diego over to second.

Coral steps in. She's not small, but she doesn't have Anna's heft. Her hair is short and straight, and she's got a compact body with wide hips. The first pitch nicks her on the arm, and she trots down to first.

So here's my big chance to be a hero. Two on, one out, score tied and all that. This pitcher's had my number all game, but like I said, he's tiring.

As long as I don't hit into a double play, we'll be fine. Anna's up next and she's barely made an out all day. She must have been some kind of star down at UMass.

He throws one of those sinkers that had us confounded in the first inning, and I swing and miss. The second pitch is low and inside. The third is a fastball, right down the middle, and I get good wood on it and line it just left of second base.

The shortstop dives and gets his glove on it, but it rolls away and I easily reach first. Diego holds at third so the game is still tied. The catcher and first baseman walk toward the mound again.

The first baseman stays there and starts throwing warm-up pitches. The pitcher walks over toward first.

"'Bout time I hit one off you," I say.

He shakes his head and kicks gently at the base. "You're new?"

"This summer."

"Who's this dyke?" he asks, jutting his chin toward Anna.

"A customer. Star of the tournament so far."

"She's not an employee?"

"No. Nobody said she has to be. I mean, to play."

"I know. Everybody on our team is, though."

"Maybe we'll make her an honorary waitress."

The new pitcher waves to the umpire that he's ready, and Anna steps into the batter's box. I take a short lead off the base and drop my arms. My mouth feels very dry.

She takes one outside pitch, then wallops the next one high and deep. I hear the first baseman say, "Son of a bitch," as he turns and watches it sail over the fence. One pitch, four runs. This thing is all but sewn up now.

Hector has pitched twenty innings today. He hugs me as I reach the bench and says, "Think we're safe?"

"Should be."

He decides to take himself out of the game and sends Alex up to pinch-hit. Jack will take the mound for the final inning and I'll move to second base. Sal goes in to catch.

Jack walks a couple of batters but nobody hits the ball out of the infield. When Coral makes the long throw across the diamond to Anna for the final out, we storm the bench and lift Hector up high. Bernie and Kyle pick up the tub of water (there's no ice left) and dump it over his shoulders.

I look around for Mercy. She's standing a few feet away.

"How's your face?" she asks.

"You tell me." I turn my head so she can examine it.

"Very ugly."

"I guess I should wash it."

"I wasn't looking at the cut," she says.

"Funny." I reach gingerly for the wound, feeling its stickiness as it tries to heal.

She tears open a Wet-Nap with a lobster picture on it and hands it to me. "We go through crates of these at the restaurant," she says.

I rub my face and it stings a bit. The wipe comes away tinged with dirt and blood.

"Want another one?" she asks.

"Sure. Nine o'clock, right?"

"Sounds good."

"Outside the bar?"

"How about at Fancy That?"

"Okay. I'll see you in an hour or so."

Hector is sitting on the bench as I walk past, the championship trophy at his side. His hair is dripping wet, but he's already put on a dry shirt.

"Great game," I say.

"They want a rematch." He sets his glove on the bench and stands. "Are you in a hurry?"

"Yeah. I gotta shower and get ready."

"Well, please stop by my place before you meet her."

"How come?"

"We *have* to do something with that hair." He's got his hands on his hips and is staring me down. Then he reaches toward my head and tries to flatten my hair. He smiles in a way that makes me uncomfortable, as if he's bestowing sweetness on me. "It's all *over* the place."

"It'll settle down after I wash it."

"Believe me. Just give me half a minute with some gel. You'll thank me later."

"Okay."

"You know the building, right? It's apartment 3-B."

"I know it." It's a faded-brick building just off Shore Road, with an art gallery and a gourmet-food store on the bottom floor and apartments above. I'm hoping this won't be some last-ditch effort to try to win me over. Turn me into a switch-hitter after all. But I'll stop by and humor him, I suppose.

I walk off the field. A red pickup truck goes by. Mercy leans out the window and gives me a wave. Her brother's driving. Hope she didn't see Hector putting his hands all over me.

Jack is already in the shower when I reach the apartment. I take a jar of peanut butter from the cupboard and dip pretzels in it for dinner, finishing the last three ounces of a carton of orange juice and downing two glasses of water. I'll get some real food somewhere with Mercy.

Jack walks into the kitchen with just a towel around his waist. He raises his fists and says, "Champions!" Considering how little real exercise he gets, he's got quite a bit of lean muscle. I guess he's so wired all the time that he couldn't possibly put on any fat.

"We kicked butt," I say.

"You celebrating tonight?"

"I'm meeting that girl, remember?"

"I do. Guess I'll hit the town. Not often I have a free evening."

"Last one for a while."

"Till after Labor Day for me."

He lights a cigarette, then steps onto the deck to smoke it. He stands there for a few seconds, then glances down at the busy courtyard café, remembers how he's "dressed," and says, "Jesus!" jumping back into the kitchen.

"Nice one," I say, cracking up.

He throws the cigarette into the sink and leans against the counter, laughing his ass off. "Shit," he says. "I hope nobody calls the cops."

"Like they'd do anything," I say. Most of the summer cops aren't much older than I am. They ride around on bicycles in gray T-shirts with POLICE in big black letters.

"I know the chief," he says, flipping his hand. "Jesus, how did I do that? With nothing but a frickin' towel on."

I eat one more pretzel, then tell him I'm going to shower. I motion toward the porch. "Tell them I'll be out in a minute for the second show."


My hair is short and fine, so I just let it air-dry as I walk over to Hector's. I decided on sandals and long khaki shorts, plus a yellow-and-blue-checked shirt with short sleeves.

"Hmmm," Hector says, sizing me up. "You going to a church supper or something, Danny?"

"Didn't know there was one."

He raises his eyebrows. "That's your best shirt?"

"Yeah."

"It's very wrinkled. And not exactly hip. Come with me."

Classical music is coming from his bedroom—I think it's Mozart. I follow him toward it; it isn't a long walk. There's no real kitchen—just a microwave and a mini-refrigerator on a counter piled high with magazines and catalogs in a sort of hallway, with a bathroom off that on one side and his bedroom on the other.

There are three or four folded shirts on top of his dresser; they appear to be brand-new. He picks up a black polo shirt with a little alligator stitched on the chest. "Let's try this," he says. He reaches for my shirt and starts unbuttoning it.

"I got it," I say, taking a step back and finishing the buttons myself. I set my shirt on the bed—it's a queen or a king and takes up nearly all of the space, neatly made with a cream-colored bedspread and a bunch of pillows.

I put the new one on and it fits. "Did you just buy this?" I ask.

"Yes, but it's okay. Just wash it and get it back to me." He reconsiders this and decides I should give it back unwashed. "You have to do these just right. You can't dump them in with your underwear and dry the life out of them."

He hits me with a spray of cologne before I know what's coming, then sweeps a few fingers over the side of my head. "Not *too* bad," he says. He picks up a large white tube—the label says L'ORÉAL STUDIO LINE—and squirts some clear gel onto his palm.

He holds it up for me to look at. "You want the size of a dime," he says. "You didn't know that, did you?"

"I've never used gel on my hair."

"I didn't think so." He rubs his palms together, then pushes the front of my hair up and off my forehead. He runs his fingers above my temples, then pats the hair down a bit and steps back.

"Great," he says.

I glance at the mirror. It's different, but not extreme. You can barely tell, actually. "Looks better," I say. "Listen, you left me hanging about whatever happened with your father. Did you work that out?"

Hector starts drumming his fingers on his thigh and looks at the floor. "We didn't talk for almost a year. Then he called me on my birthday this past April and *kind of* tried to be nice. Asked how I've been doing in this very vague way, and seemed glad when I told him I was fine. He has no idea that you can be gay and be happy and be *connected* to someone."

"Right."

"Not that I *am* connected. But I *could* be. . . . My father just thinks everybody has to toe some narrow path."

I look in the mirror again. Funny how we both have this *dis*-connect with our fathers and a *need* to connect with a partner. We're disconnected from our fathers in very different ways—him because of his father's irrational anger and me out of my father's benign slack. That's a much wider gap than the fact that Hector wants a male partner and I want a girlfriend.

"So," he says, "did you decide where to take her?"

"No. She's local. I figured she'd know what to do."

The CD has ended. He reaches for the player—on a small bedside table with a white lamp—and restarts it. "That new gelato place is great."

"What's that?"

"It's like ice cream, but better. And I think Maine Street is underage until ten. They have pool tables and video games."

"Sounds like a possibility," I say. I step out of the bedroom and lean against the wall in the hallway. "I was gonna see if she'd want some pizza. I haven't eaten much. . . . Where are you going?"

"We're heading to the Front Porch."

"The team?"

"Yeah. And some other people from work."

"They check IDs over there?" I ask.

"Very definitely."

"Then that leaves us out."

"Well, maybe stop back later. I might end up here with some people. You never know. Anything can happen in Ogunquit."

I get out of there in a hurry; I have this vague feeling that I'm starting to break his heart, but there's nothing I can do to help him.

I'm a few minutes early, but Mercy is already waiting on a bench outside Fancy That. She stands and says, "Hi," which is no big deal in itself, but she says it in a way that indicates she's glad to see me. I wasn't so sure she would be after my comment this afternoon about her butt.

She says pizza is fine with her, so we cross the street and wait on the sidewalk twenty minutes for a table. The restaurant is up a flight of stairs and there's a large deck area, filled with families and couples and groups of guys. We can hear the karaoke from the bar next door. The street is crammed with people walking and eating ice cream and going in and out of the shops, which stay open until at least eleven, even on a Tuesday, now that summer's here.

"You look cool," she says, taking a step back and looking me over.

"I didn't before?"

"I didn't say *that*. But, you know, that's a really nice shirt. And you did something with your hair. Or *some*body did."

She's wearing a gray T-shirty thing—better than a T-shirt, but similar; fitted and ribbed—and jeans. Lipstick just a shade or so darker than her lips. And her hair is down and flowing to her shoulders; no ponytail tonight.

"You look great," I say. I appreciate that she's gone to some effort to look good for our date. Obviously Hector was right to fuss over me, too.

I nod up toward the pizza place. "Did you hang out here as a kid?"

She shrugs. "Not so much. There are tourist places and there are 'local' places."

"And this is a tourist place?"

"In summer it is. Not that that's so bad—it's just *crowded*, obviously. When you live here, you know which places to avoid in season."

"Do you natives hate it when the tourists come to town?"

"Not really. This town would have nothing without the summer. But yeah, you brace yourself in late spring when you know they're coming, and you *love* it in September when you get your town back. The autumn visitors are mostly older. And straight."

A waitress calls to us from the deck, and we go up and sit at an outdoor table. She asks us what we want to drink, and I say, "A Coke," not waiting for Mercy to order first.

"I'll have a Coors Light," she says. I know she's only twenty, but the waitress doesn't even ask. I probably could have had one, too. I'd never drink anything light, but a Molson or even a regular Coors would beat the hell out of a Coke.

Mercy leans forward and whispers, "She was a year ahead of Faith in high school and always confuses us. So she thinks I'm, like, twenty-three."

"So you do come here?"

"Occasionally."

"What's good? I don't eat cheese."

"The pizza is awesome. The crust, I mean. You can get it without cheese. Most of the toppings are good. . . . Your face looks better."

"It stings."

"It's a clean cut. Might leave a little scar."

"I guess that'll make me look tough."

"Scary."

We eat, then try the gelato place, then sit on a bench by Fancy That and watch people go by for an hour.

"So," she says, "you followed your father up here for the summer?"

"Something like that." I'm looking at her throat—that space below her ear, specifically, where the jaw curves away and there's a tender, vertical ridge of neck muscle that would fit neatly between my lips. "He'd been after me to come up. Reconnect, you know."

She sees that I'm staring and tilts her head slightly to block my view. "Is it working?"

"Not really." I swallow a buildup of saliva and turn my attention to her very cute little ear. "He acts like we're both eighteen or something."

She slowly shakes her head. "*Mine* act like I'm twelve. They think I'm at my girlfriend's tonight watching TV."

I learn a bit more about her: she lived on a fairly wild dorm floor as a freshman and overcompensated for what she called her "puritanical high-school years," getting drunk, smoking pot, and having sex—all for the first time. By February she'd had enough of that and started spending her evenings in the library.

Mostly we just joke around and observe the crowd. By midnight the pace has slowed considerably—the families have gone off to bed—but the bar-hoppers are still out in force.

I'm wondering how Hector's doing, so I mention to Mercy that there might be a team party going on.

"And you want to go?" Doesn't sound like she wants to.

"Maybe for a few minutes. I said I would. I kind of feel obligated."

"Why?"

"I just do."

She shrugs. "Okay. For a few minutes."

I can see from the street that the lights are on up there, so we climb the stairs and I knock on the door. I hear laughter, but it doesn't sound like a big crowd.

Hector has his shirt off when he answers the door—he has no pecs and virtually no chest hair. He smiles, but his "Hello" lacks some of his usual enthusiasm. He opens the door farther but doesn't step aside to let us in.

"You said to stop by," I say. "Remember?"

"Oh . . . yeah. But . . . you know, nobody else really showed up."

"Hi, Danny." It's Chase, coming out of the bathroom.

"Hey." I look over at Mercy, who has an embarrassed smile.

"Oh," I say, "this is Mercy. So . . . nothing much going on, huh?"

"No." Hector shakes his head. Chase has come up behind him and put both hands on Hector's shoulders. "They all stayed at the Porch, so . . ."

Chase finishes Hector's sentence. "So we just came back here to relax."

"Well," I say, "then we won't, you know . . ."

"Oh, stay." Hector steps aside now to let us in. "Have a drink."

"No. That's okay."

"It's all right," Mercy says, staying put. "Danny thought there might be a party."

"Oh," Hector says. "We said there might be, but . . ."

"Listen," I say, "it's no big deal."

"You sure?"

"Sure. We'll see you tomorrow."

"Okay. Good night."

I walk ahead of her down the stairs and onto the sidewalk.

"God," she says when we're definitely out of earshot.

"I know."

"Wonder what *they're* planning to do."

"You think?"

"Come on," she says. "What do *you* think?"

I know what I think. And I'm a little surprised. Chase acts like he'll do anybody, but Hector seemed more judicious than that.

"I'm not sure I trust Chase," I say.

"Why not?"

"I don't know."

"What do you care?"

"I don't."

The night is clear, so I'm thinking the moonrise thing Hector pulled on me might be a good trick. So I say, "Let's go down by the water."

We turn past the Sparhawk and onto the Marginal Way. The moon is definitely not up, but how much longer could it take?

We sit on the same bench I sat on with Hector, and I watch for the orange glow of the moon. It's warmer out than it was that night.

"My brother said he saw you late one night walking with that guy."

"With Hector?"

"The dark one."

"So?"

"He's *cute*, isn't he?"

"I don't know. He's a *guy*."

"Well, Buddy was wondering what you were interested in *me* for."

I turn to face her. "I'm not gay."

"I didn't say you were."

"I'm *not*."

"He said he'd kill you if I got AIDS."

I start to say something about Buddy being an asshole, but I remember in a hurry that he's her brother, so I don't. But I certainly say it loud and clear to myself. What I ask aloud is, "What did *you* say?"

"I told him he has nothing to worry about."

I'm not sure what that means. That she's certain I'm clean or that there's no way I'll be sleeping with her?

"You got a problem with gay people?" I ask.

Her answer is sharp. "No. I have a problem with people who can't figure themselves out."

"You mean me?"

"You're always hanging around with these . . ." She stops short, searching for a word.

"These what?"

"These gay people."

"Yeah. Say what you really mean. These what?"

"I *said* what I mean. I don't call them queers or faggots like my brother does. This isn't homophobia. It's about whether I can trust you."

"Trust *me*?"

"Look," she says. "I went out with this basketball player at school for a couple of months. I think I slept with him twice; the only person I've *ever* slept with. Then I find out he's sleeping with some *guy* at the same time. Going back and forth. He didn't tell me shit; I found out about it from his roommate."

"What'd you do?"

"I punched him in the mouth. Then I went and got tested and sweated that out until the results came. I was clean, okay, but that was criminal, if you ask me. The scumbag. So, yeah, Buddy has nothing to worry about. I've been through that risk already."

I don't ask the obvious questions. Are you celibate? Do you avoid guys you think might consider going both ways? Is it okay as long as I wear a condom? Maybe two or three? Should I write off that possibility right now?

"*I'm* not confused," I say.

"You seemed really flirty with that Hector during the softball games."

"He's a nice guy. He's very funny. We *work* together; that's the only reason I know him."

"And it doesn't bother you that he's going down on that other guy right this minute?"

"Why would it bother me?"

"It seemed to."

"It *didn't.*"

"Then why'd we go to his apartment?"

It's a good question, and I don't have an answer just yet. I don't like thinking about what they're up to, but it's their business. I think Hector can do better than that, but so what?

There's still no sign of the moon, but I sure don't feel romantic anyway. She's got her arms folded and is a couple of feet away from me. We stare at the ocean for a little while, then she says she ought to be getting home.

We don't say much on the way back. We get to Shore Road and make a left and she stops at the next corner.

"Our house is up this street," she says.

"Okay."

"So I'll see you around," she says.

"I'll walk you up."

"I'm fine. It's, like, fifty yards."

"Okay. I'll see ya."

That sure ended abruptly. I just make a stupid pointing motion at her with my finger and back away, like I'm cool.

Which I'm not.

So I walk past our place and out to the main street, wondering what Chase and Hector are up to without letting myself go into detail. I don't care what they're doing as much as how they're feeling about each other. Hector's vulnerable and Chase has no soul, so that's a dead end if I ever saw one.

What if you could take Hector's humor and amiability and cross it with Mercy's looks and her body? Wouldn't be a bad mix, I'd say.

But if you took her sometimes acidic demeanor and meshed it with Hector's physicality? I wouldn't go near it for anything.

So where does that leave me?

Right back where I started.

# 7

## "Sooner or later, something sticks."

**"Y**ou see the paper?" Hector asks as soon as I enter the kitchen the next night.

"No. What paper?"

"*The York County News.*"

"Big deal."

"*Look* at it." He holds up the front page, where there's a fairly large photo of some of us celebrating on the field after the softball tournament.

I look at the picture. Hector is triumphantly holding the trophy aloft with one hand and has the other one around Chase's neck. Chase is leaning with both arms around Hector's waist, and Sal is behind Chase with one fist raised. They're all beaming at the camera. Just to the side you can see Anna hugging Diego, and I appear to be glaring at Hector and Chase, looking like I'm pissed off. I have no recollection of that moment or of being in a sour mood. The camera must have caught me in the instant of an expression change, giving a false impression that I was annoyed.

"I bought six copies," Hector says. "Isn't it a great picture?"

"Very cool," I say. A real highlight. I'll have to buy a dozen to send back home. *Dear Grandma. Here's a picture of me and my new gay friends.*

The night goes slowly, probably because I don't feel like being here. I keep to myself, scrubbing the pots, loading and unloading the dishwasher, carrying cases of beer and wine upstairs, taking the garbage out to the Dumpster.

Hector keeps coming in and looking at me. He asks me what's wrong for about the fourth time, and I say nothing, just tired.

"You don't look tired," he says. "And you never told me how it went with that girl."

"It was okay," I say.

"Just okay?"

"Just okay."

I turn back to the sink and resume scrubbing. He goes back upstairs to rake in the tips.

"You seem really distant," he says about an hour later.

"I'm right here," I reply.

"You know what I mean. You're in some zone."

So here's what I figured out while sitting around the apartment today and zoning out at work. Yeah, it bothered me when I discovered Hector with Chase. If he's attracted to me, then he should stoically accept that I'll never be available to him and not use Chase as some second-rate alternative. And when Mercy challenged me about it, she was way off base, but maybe she was sort of right in a parallel kind of way. And my reaction to her reaction managed to botch up my chances with her, too.

Jack gets home before I do, which I can't remember happening before. He's sitting in the dark on the deck. "Grab a beer," he says. "I brought home a case of Heineken."

So I take one of the green bottles from the refrigerator and open the screen door. The café below us is closed, but there's a light on in the kitchen and somebody's still working in there. Probably mopping the floor, like I just did.

"Long night," Jack says.

"They all are."

"Take a load off. . . . You liking it here?"

"Yeah," I say. I'm still not sure if that's true. I take a swig of the beer. I'm not much of a drinker, but this tastes perfect considering the hour and the hard work behind me. And my mood.

"The people are cool, huh?" he says.

"They are."

The air is comfortably warm and moving minimally; it's never quite still this close to the water. Jack is wearing his dark sunglasses even though the sun went down about six hours ago. "Good to have you here," he says. I've been here almost a month, but we haven't spent much time just sitting together and talking. He's always doing something.

"Yeah. It's been a while." That's not quite the way to put it;

I've *never* been here before this summer. But there hadn't been any visits—me to him or him to me—for a couple of years.

"They're treating you good, though. Right?"

By "they," he means my grandparents. They've raised me mostly. Or at least they put up some hazy kind of barriers or safety nets so I wouldn't go too far off course.

"I have no complaints."

I think he's fishing around to see if I have any resentment over his long absences. I've never expected much from him; I probably learned that at birth. I don't spend much energy relying on other people. Sooner or later, they all let you down. But I get the feeling he's been thinking about what I said a while back, how he's never around for me. That's probably why he waited up tonight.

I take another sip of the beer and set it on the plastic table. He's eyeing me carefully, squinting a bit and smiling. He leans forward and his voice is softer than usual. "Think of yourself, right now—you're almost twenty—think how your life would be if you had a two-year-old like I did at your age."

Right, but he wasn't exactly tied down like some young dads. He wasn't changing diapers or tucking me in or supporting me in any real way.

Maybe he senses what I'm thinking, because he owns up to it a bit.

"Yeah, I was lucky," he says, sitting back. He studies the label of his beer bottle for a few seconds. "Al and Barbara"—my mother's parents—"were cool. I mean, they were *pissed*—don't get me wrong—but they're the sort who take things in stride and . . . well, Al came to my house and we sat at the table with *my* parents, and he said if I'd do what I could to be a dad—be a part of your life, pitch in for clothes and hang out with you regularly, all that stuff—then they'd share the real parenting with your mom and not hold my feet to the fire. I mean, it wasn't like we were in *love.* No way we were getting married or that I would move in. Nobody wanted that. They sure didn't. So what was I supposed to do? I'm a senior in high school and I'm looking at a choice between a life sentence or probation, basically. So I took probation."

"And Mom took the life sentence."

"She wanted to *keep* you, Danny. So, yeah, it was like two nights a week or so, I have to go, 'Sorry, guys, I can't smoke dope tonight and hang outside Chicken Delight until it closes; I have to play LEGOs with my kid.'"

"Tough break, Dad." So he *didn't* want me to be "kept"?

"I loved it; you know that. It *took* a while. And I started resenting Al being the main guy in your life. But now I know he did us all a major-league favor. No way was I ready to be a father; I was more like a big brother or an uncle. But once I got into it, I loved it, man. It makes me happy as hell that you turned out okay, that you're happy and not messed up. I *do* care. Hell, you're in college."

"Not quite."

"You'll go back. Shit, I barely finished high school. That's nothing. I worried for years that I was screwing you up by being a lousy role model. You hear all this stuff about absent fathers . . .

that scared the shit out of me." His voice is a little more urgent now, but still quiet, still much more measured than I've ever heard from him at Dishes.

"You did all right," I say.

"When I was with you, I tried to be the best father I could. I know there were gaps in there . . . but I never stopped thinking about you."

"I turned out okay." He already said that about me, but he's right.

"It made me so frickin' happy when you said you'd come up here for the summer. *So* frickin' happy. Like maybe now that we're both adults . . . I don't know. I'm no more mature than you are. I just know a lot of shit."

That makes me laugh. "Yeah, you do."

"It never stops, you know. It's not like you hit some age and all of a sudden you know everything and you coast. *Women* you never figure out. Finances either. Politics, religion, who's gonna win the Super Bowl. I can't even figure out how to shut up. I just keep talking and sooner or later, something sticks."

He finishes his beer and gets up to grab another one. "You good?" he asks.

I check my bottle and it's half full. "I'm good."

Jack isn't much of a drinker, either. He's said bartenders who drink just get themselves in trouble.

He's gone a few minutes, using the bathroom, I suppose. It feels like we broke some ice. When he comes back, the sunglasses are off. His eyes are bloodshot, probably from lack of sleep.

I ask him something I've been wanting to know. "How come you work in a gay bar?"

"How come *you* do?"

"Because you got me the job."

He laughs. "It's the best place in town. Great money. And I love the people. I don't give a shit who they sleep with. Do you?"

Some of them. But I shake my head. "No. . . . Straight people ever give you a hard time about it?"

He shrugs. "Screw them. Yeah. I don't give a shit. I've had some fights. . . . This town is basically cool. Us liberals way out-number the jerks."

The lights go off in the café's kitchen. I drink the last few ounces of my beer and shut my eyes, enjoying the warm air. When I open my eyes, he's looking at me, looking satisfied and maybe proud.

"One more question," I say. "If you'd had your way twenty years ago, I wouldn't be here, right? I never would have been *any-where.*"

He chews on his lip and glances in the direction of the ocean, which we can't see because of the inns and the churches and the trees. "Let's just say smarter heads prevailed. No—I didn't push for anything like that. It just seemed like a viable option when I first heard about you. When your mom missed her period. You weren't *Danny* then. You weren't my son. I was *seventeen,* man. I didn't know what it'd be like."

He stands up and squeezes my shoulder.

"I understand," I say. "I never even thought about that until now."

It's strange, realizing that it would have been an easy thing to eliminate me. Maybe I'd be around in some other incarnation by now. Maybe I never would have been.

"Now I want another beer," I say. "You staying up?"

"Yeah. I'll get it."

"Maybe grab my sweatshirt, too?"

"Sure. It's already after three. We might as well hang out and watch the sun come up. How often in life do you get to do that?"

He comes back wearing a baggy blue sweater, carrying a package of pretzels, my sweatshirt, and a fat cigar, which he lights and sets in the ashtray. He puts his feet on the deck railing and folds his arms. "Can sleep all morning," he says.

"Yeah."

"So how *is* your mom?"

"Seems okay. Stoic, I guess."

"Doesn't get out much?"

"Other than work? No."

"Never dates?"

"Not that I know of."

He picks up the cigar and takes a long drag. It must seem so long ago to him that they were together. More than half his life. But he seems to have some regrets. That he moved on and she couldn't.

I start to ask a question, but stop. "How many times—?"

"What?"

"Nothing."

"How many times what?"

"Forget it."

He smiles, gives me an amused but slightly scornful look. "With her? Not many."

"Oh."

"I mean, I guess it depends on how you define it. In the Bill Clinton definition, we 'had sex' maybe four times. By the American-high-school-teenager definition, maybe thirty."

I just nod. Hard to picture my mom that way, and I guess I'd prefer not to.

"She was cute," he says.

She isn't anymore. Way overweight, never smiles much.

"Why do you want to know?" he asks.

"I don't know. . . . Something about opportunity. Some notion I've had that we all have one tiny shot at being who we are—at being *at all*—and that the odds against us ever coming to life are beyond calculation."

"Deep." He nods slowly.

I *am* feeling deep. I can count on one hand the times I've had a philosophical discussion with anyone, so maybe this has all been stuck in my brain wanting to get out. "Every once in a while a sperm actually reaches its target, but billions of them just die. Somehow *me*—the me inside that sperm—somehow made it. And if I hadn't been in the right stream, if I hadn't outswam all the others, if I'd been shot out in the shower or into some other opening, I'd never have been me. There might have been another person *like* me—same parents, same hair color, same speech pattern, same beliefs even. But it wouldn't be *me*. Not *my* consciousness, not *my* personality.

"Just think about the percentages," I continue. "The odds against being here. Being alive."

"It's a trip, ain't it?"

"It's something else."

We're quiet then, and we both doze off in the plastic chairs. A while later a couple of guys walk by on the street, talking louder than they should. I'm pretty sure one of the voices is Chase.

Jack sits forward and rubs out his cigar. I blink a few times.

"You getting anywhere with that girl?" he asks.

I look at him and shake my head back and forth about a quarter inch to either side. "Don't know," I say. "She seems . . . untrusting."

"You barely know her, right?"

"Right."

"There's plenty of women out there."

"Not in this town."

He laughs. "I hear you. But she seemed worth pursuing."

Obviously. Since he once did.

"I'll keep at it," I say. "Did you visit Arnie when you were in the Bahamas last winter?"

"Yeah. I stayed at his place. We hit the casino every night. Best trip I ever had."

"You win?"

"I came out ahead. Didn't hurt that I had a free place to stay and Arnie paid for all the food. He insisted."

"Didn't want anything in return?"

"Just a friend." He looks directly at me. "No strings whatso-ever."

"That's good." I'm still wondering what strings Hector's friendship might entail.

By five we're getting chilled, so we put on jackets and walk over to the Marginal Way. The weather is clear—should be a great sunrise.

It's Thursday in Ogunquit. Daybreak.

## 8

# "I like walking around all night."

I figure three thirty has to be the slowest time at the Haddock Shack—too late for lunch and too early for dinner. But most of the tables are full, and there's as much steam as ever coming from the kitchen.

I take a seat and glance at the ads on the placemat: Sunrise Properties, Studio East Motel, The Ogunquit Playhouse. Four old ladies behind me are talking about the chowder. One says it's exactly the same here as it was in the 1950s. Another says it's *nothing* like it was back then. "The clams were sweeter and more tender then. And they used richer cream. And paprika."

"There's paprika in this."

"Not as much."

Mercy slides into the other side of my booth. Different shirt today; it's red with a silver lobster. She's wearing a black hair band instead of the ponytail. Picked up a tan, too.

"Here for breakfast?" she asks. She thinks she's joking.

"Kind of. Stayed up all night with my father and slept until two."

"Nice schedule. So why *are* you here?"

"Because I hear the chowder's good."

"It is."

"Maybe I'll have some."

"Well, I'm on my break. You'll have to wait for Gail."

"No problem."

She slides back out of the booth. "I'm kidding. I mean, I *am* on break, but I'll get whatever you want."

"Okay. Chowder and iced tea."

She comes back with two bowls of the soup and sits next to me this time.

"Let's see the wound," she says.

I haven't even thought about it much. I turn my head and she looks it over, touching it gently with her fingertips. "Healing nicely. . . . So what'd you do yesterday?"

"I don't know. Ran and worked. Drank a couple of beers last night and watched the sun come up." And thought about whether her good points outweigh the negatives.

She opens a package of oyster crackers and pours them into her bowl, looking straight ahead. "Didn't call me."

"No."

"Supposed to after a date. Right?"

"I don't know. I didn't think it ended so great."

She shrugs. "Me either."

I stir the chowder, which seems plenty creamy to me, and add some pepper. "Didn't know if you'd want to hear from me."

She presses her thigh against mine. "I did. . . . I believed what you said. About not being confused."

The soup tastes pretty good. I've probably tasted the chowder at six different places up here, and it's all been good. I'd say this one is average for Ogunquit.

"So let's see," she says. "I work eleven to nine six days a week, and you work what, five to two?"

"Something like that."

"So a second date would take place, say, at three in the morning? Assuming I took a nap after work?"

"I guess so."

She feigns disappointment. "Nothing's open then."

"That's a predicament."

"Isn't it, though?" She reaches for my iced tea and takes a massive sip through the straw. "Okay if I have some of this?" she asks after finishing.

"No."

"Okay. I'll put it back." She takes the glass again and leans over it with her mouth open.

I grab her wrist and push the glass away.

"So I'm off on Tuesday again," she says.

"Not me."

"What time do you close on Monday?"

"One."

"I could nap until midnight and then meet you when you're done."

"Sounds . . . great," I say. "Where would we go?"

She gives me that mischievous smile. "I like walking around all night."

"Me, too."

"We could have a picnic on the beach."

"I like the sound of that. We'd better check the tide schedule."

"I already did," she says. "Low tide's at two oh-seven."

"So you had this planned, huh?"

"I knew you'd be back."

"How come?"

"'Cause I'm worth it."

"You think so, huh?"

The women behind us have started up again. "I still say it hasn't changed," the first one says.

"How could it *not* have changed? Everything changes."

"It's as good as ever, Betty."

"It *isn't*."

It's nearly five when I get back to the apartment. I'm feeling like a slug because I didn't have time to run today. Could head out for a couple of miles and get to work late, but that chowder's sitting heavy in my stomach. So I just walk over to Dishes and figure one day without a workout won't kill me.

The place is already hopping; Thursday is the weekend around here come summer. The piano goes nonstop from four p.m. to closing.

Fitch sends me upstairs, where most of the action is when the sing-alongs are under way. The kitchen is very small; just a couple of large refrigerators, two sinks, and stacks of glasses in plastic trays. I'll have my hands in soapy water for the next nine hours, listening to Broadway tunes and other standards.

I haven't checked, but my guess is that there are mostly straight people around the piano right now, because I don't hear any powerful voices. They're doing "I Left My Heart in San Francisco" but just pecking away at it. Dane and Stanley and the others will be along later this evening. Some of those guys sing really well.

This kitchen is also where the waiters come to primp and bitch. Chase walks in all sweet and friendly, not even slightly embarrassed or uneasy about us catching him half-dressed with Hector. "Hi, Danny!" he says as if we were old buddies.

"Hey," I say flatly. Totally noncommittal.

And where *is* Hector, anyway? Haven't seen him yet.

I hear someone coming up the rattly back steps—it's an outside staircase, metal and uncovered—and the back kitchen door opens. Kyle comes in, looking all flustered. "God, I'm *so* late," he says.

"It's okay," Chase says. "We've got it covered." He leans over and kisses Kyle on the mouth.

Magical.

"Is Fitch downstairs?" Kyle asks.

"Yeah. Why?"

"I have to go down there and punch in. He'll be pissed."

"Tell him you've been here and just forgot," Chase says.

"Will you vouch for me?"

"If he asks."

Kyle hurries out of the kitchen.

"He's so nervous," Chase says. "So what if he's ten minutes late?"

"We have schedules," I say.

"I know, but God. This is O*gun*quit."

"So?"

He gives me a grin and sways his fingers and hips and starts singing slowly: "Summertime, and the livin' is easy."

I stick my hands back in the sink and wash some pint glasses. Chase goes out to the bar room.

"What does he *do* anyway?" I ask Hector a while later.

"Chase?"

"Yeah."

"When he's not here? He teaches high-school English in Boston."

"Oh."

"You don't like him, huh?"

"Why do you say that?"

"He seems to annoy you."

"He's a little too 'easygoing' for me."

"He just likes to have fun. It's *summer*, Danny."

"Yeah, he already told me that. . . . *Sung* it, I mean."

"He's a riot."

Yeah, I'm sure Hector would think so if he saw him kissing Kyle. Or any of the others. Or maybe Hector's just as loose with his affections. Maybe he's not so selective after all.

How do I put this? I have no interest in Hector sexually. But *he's* shown interest in *me*. So how does he have the nerve to think he'd have a chance with me—if such a chance even existed—but could screw around with some whorish guy right in front of my face? That doesn't add up.

"Did you guys have fun the other night?" I ask.

Hector looks offended. "*Dan*ny," he says.

"What?"

He makes that scolding sound again, tongue against teeth. "Don't pry."

"I'm not prying."

"Well then, yes, we had a nice time together. . . . He's a very sweet guy."

"Glad to hear it."

Hector steps closer and puts his hand around my bicep. I shrug it away.

"*Some*body's a little grumpy today," he says.

Somebody's had enough of Hector's bullshit.

I'm weary as hell when I leave work. No sleep last night, a few fitful hours on the couch during the day, and a frantic pace all night in the kitchen. I stink and I'm greasy and I'm wired from two bottles of Mountain Dew.

So I spread out on the floor in front of my couch and alternate sets of push-ups and sit-ups for half an hour. Then I take a long hot shower and finish the bag of pretzels. It's 2:54. Where the hell does Jack go on these nights he doesn't come home?

He's obviously not alone out there. Like I am. Good for him, I guess.

Then again, Mercy's giving me another chance. I'll take it.

Better start getting some sleep. I've got another all-nighter in a few days.

Summertime. So far it hasn't been easy.

# "All he ever wants is a walk and his dinner."

Forty miles in four days: a hilly ten on Friday on the back roads west of Ogunquit, eight up through Wells and back along the beach on Saturday, fourteen very early Sunday before the heat descended, and eight more all-out this morning up in Israel Head and Pine Hill.

I also took a nap this afternoon, so I'm ready for anything.

The place has been absolutely jammed all night. She comes to the kitchen door about quarter to one. It's still very warm out, but she's wearing the Addison sweatshirt and has a small knapsack. Her smile is sweet and shy.

Things have been more or less back to normal with Hector all weekend, whatever normal means. Joking around during his quick twenty-second breathers. I catch him giving me his wistful looks, but I've also seen him leaving with Chase a couple of times.

I finish up. We close at one, but there'll be a big wave of

glassware to wash. Sergei said he'd take care of all that, so I'll be out of here in a few minutes.

I desperately need a shower and some flossing.

"Up here," I say as we reach the apartment. We go around back and climb the wooden steps. "I just need to get washed up."

She grabs a magazine and sits on the couch.

We need a new bar of soap; this one is greenish-gray and worn down to a flimsy sliver.

After my shower I find Jack leaning against the kitchen counter and Mercy sitting at the table with one of those Heinekens. The Little League photo from the refrigerator is sitting on the table.

"Hey, boy," Jack says, giving me a knowing smile.

Mercy tilts her head. "Jack was telling me about New Jersey."

"What about it?"

"Well, I've never been there. You hear all these awful things."

"Like how grungy it is?"

"Yeah. . . . But he makes it sound nice."

I look at Jack with a half grimace. "He must have been lying."

"It ain't like here," Jack says.

Mercy holds up the Little League picture. "Cute," she says.

"Sure." I turn to Jack. "Why *is* that here?"

He takes it from Mercy and holds it up, squinting to see it better. "It's the only picture I have with both of us in it," he says. He sets it down and addresses her. "Absent dads only get the B-list stuff. All the baby pictures and that shit are at his mom's."

I never realized that the photo was actually meaningful to him.

"I can get you more pictures," I say. "Next time I go home."

"That'd be great," he says. "There's one on the beach when you were about four. Down in Belmar. You're in this giant hole you dug in the sand and I'm handing you a shovel and a bottle of Coke. Haven't seen that in years."

"How'd you remember it?"

He shrugs. "I don't know. I gave it to your grandfather. Thought he'd get a kick out of it. It always stuck in my head. . . . So, what are you guys up to?"

"A picnic," Mercy says, "on the beach."

Jack looks from her, to me, to her, then nods. "Good time of night for it. Better put on some sunblock."

"He works all evening and I work all day," Mercy says.

"Doesn't leave much time for fun, does it?" Jack pushes away from the counter and rubs his hands together. "Speaking of which . . . I've got an appointment of my own."

"You're going out in the middle of the night?" I ask.

"Yep. Just stopped here for a shower."

"What's open?"

"Nothing. Going to her place."

"*Who?*"

"You haven't met her. Soon."

I yank open a drawer and pull out fresh socks and a couple of shirts. Mercy gets up and sits next to me on the couch.

Jack heads for the bathroom. "See you tomorrow, I guess. Nice to see you, Mercy."

"You, too."

He stays in the doorway for a few seconds, looking at her.

She looks back. "You *do* remember me, don't you?"

Jack thinks it over. "Yeah. . . . Okay?"

She shrugs gently. "Sure."

He juts his head toward me. "You're better off with this guy."

She giggles. "I don't know about *that.*"

He opens his palms and makes a sheepish gesture. "How would I know you'd meet my son?"

"How would I know you'd *have* one?"

I look at her now and can't hide the very puzzled look on my face. I wait until I hear the shower running. "Two minutes on the beach?"

"Maybe it was twenty. It was *two years* ago. He's an interesting guy, Danny. Believe me, it never went beyond talking."

"But he wanted it to."

"I'm sure he did. What guy *doesn't* want it to go beyond talking? He wasn't creepy or anything . . . just a little out of my age range."

"You were in high school."

"I'd graduated."

"You said it was two minutes."

"Well, I didn't want you thinking I *let* myself get hit on by old guys. I mean, I almost never get picked up on the beach. Maybe a couple of times a week. And usually not by anyone over thirty."

She sees my astonishment and starts laughing. "I'm kidding, you idiot. What do you think I am?"

"I think you're . . . a bit of a tease."

She picks up her knapsack. "Come on, I've got turkey sand-wiches and coleslaw. . . . What are you bringing?"

Condoms. Maybe a couple of those Heinekens. "A blanket? So we don't have to sit on the sand?"

"That'll work. Dress warm. You'll be surprised how cold it gets."

We walk back toward the business area. A few of the bars are still open. Hector comes out of the Front Porch a half block ahead of us. He sees us coming and stops.

"You haven't seen Chase, have you?" he asks.

"No," I say. "We just got out here."

"Did he leave work early?" He's looking blankly at Mercy, but I answer.

"I think he was still there when I left."

Hector frowns and rubs his hands against his thighs, looking up the street toward the theater. "Well, he slipped out before I was done. . . . We were *supposed* to have a drink after."

"I guess something came up."

He sighs. "Yeah. Something always seems to."

"Well, we're headed for the beach. Guess we'll see you tomor-row."

"Have fun."

Mercy adjusts the knapsack on her shoulder and puts her hand on my back as we walk. "He's lovesick, huh?" Her tone is slightly sarcastic.

"I don't know. I told you, Chase is a bit of a jerk."

"Such melodrama. Besides, I'm not sure it's Chase he's after."

"What makes you say that?"

"He looks at me like I'm his main rival or something."

"For me?"

"You never can tell." Her hand slips down my back. "I think he knows a great guy when he meets one."

"I feel for him."

"Okay, fine. But I don't think he was looking for Chase."

My hands are free, so I put one on her back and we cross the bridge over the river. The ocean is straight ahead of us; the river hooks around and forms a little peninsula here, with a parking lot to the right and a couple of small motels and restaurants to the left, mostly facing the ocean. There's a van and a station wagon parked next to each other in the lot; otherwise it's empty.

"Speaking of parents," she says, "do you have any relationship with your mom?"

"Yeah. Of course. It's not a *great* relationship, but I call her every Sunday morning."

"That's good. It can't be easy being a mom at seventeen."

"She's thirty-eight."

"You know what I mean."

The beach is more typical here, a flat sandy area. At high tide there's not more than twenty feet between the parking lot and the water, but right now the sea is a hundred yards away.

"We should leave our shoes here," she says, bending over to untie her running shoes. "Otherwise they'll get full of sand."

We walk to where the river and the ocean meet. We're less than thirty yards from the rocks and the Marginal Way, but you'd have to cross a swift-moving channel to get there.

From this point you can look up the beach toward Wells to the north or over into Ogunquit across the river. The huge Ontio and Lookout condominium buildings are at the highest point. Below them, the Sparhawk, Beachmere, and Anchorage resorts are spread out along the Marginal Way.

We hear the nightly rumble of thunder as we spread out the blanket. The air already feels cooler here by the water, and the breeze is stronger. She flops down on the blanket and opens a beer, propping up on her elbows. We can hear waves hitting the rocks across the river.

There are a couple of boats way out near the horizon. It's still clear out there, although it's clouding up in a hurry onshore.

As soon as we start eating sandwiches, some seagulls begin poking around a few feet away. She throws a crust of roll over their heads and they scramble for it. "Dumb move," she says. "Now they'll never leave us alone."

She sits up and crosses her legs in a lotus position. She's way more flexible than I am.

I lie back on the blanket and look up at the sky. Some stars are still visible, but most of the space above us is filled with wispy clouds. She lies down, too, and her shoulder presses into mine.

"So, Danny," she says sort of singsongy, "how do you like Ogunquit?"

"I like it fine." I press my toes against hers. They're gritty from the sand, but it gets our legs into full contact. We're both wearing jeans. "I mean, look at this. The ocean, the sky . . . you."

She giggles. She squeezes my thigh and turns toward me. I turn toward her.

Now we're face-to-face, and the caressing begins to build. I close my eyes and put my face against hers, nestling my nose into her sweatshirt hood and her hair, grazing her ear with my mouth.

And just as we start making out, a strong gust of wind blows some sand across us. She turns away and wipes her mouth and sneezes. She smiles at me, waiting for the wind to die down.

"Maybe," she says, as another gust comes up, "the beach isn't the best place to be right now."

"No?"

"Let's cross over." She waves toward the Marginal Way. "Not much sand on those rocks."

"Sounds good."

Trying to cross the river would not be a good idea. We backtrack across the bridge and partway toward town, taking a path that winds through a couple of properties, and up by the Terrace by the Sea motel, right past our apartment. We ditch her knapsack under the back steps and continue up Shore Road for a ways, just carrying the blanket.

There's a flash overhead and more thunder.

"Heat lightning," I say. "Nothing to worry about."

We've got our arms around each other and stop to kiss every few steps when we reach the Marginal Way. We have to walk slowly because it's so dark out, but we both know every step of this path.

We carefully make our way down the rocks toward a flattish,

secluded spot that's more sandy dirt than rock. We're still well above the water, protected by a sort of natural rock fortress that narrows to a point. The waves are crashing fifteen feet below us as the tide comes in with force.

Mercy takes a deep inhale. "Isn't that great?"

It's the aroma of salt and seaweed and mussels and cold, rushing water. "Nothing better," I say, especially since she's got her whole body leaning into me. I'm comfortably braced against a boulder.

She puts her mouth against my face and whispers. "If you could imagine what the beginning of life would smell like, that would be it."

My hand slides along her back to that napey area at the base of her spine, just above the cleavage of her butt. Farther below, her muscles are firm and round and smooth.

The wind has increased even more and the thunder is getting closer. We can feel the air starting to crackle and the wind growing moist.

My hand moves easily over her skin. Her tongue finds its way into my mouth.

Lightning hits close by. There's a massive crack of thunder.

"This is gonna be bad," she says, adjusting her pants. "Come on!" She starts scrambling over the rocks toward the Marginal Way.

I shake my head in frustration and take off after her, feeling the first few drops of rain and the whistling of the wind. We reach the path and start sprinting for Perkins Cove.

She's laughing as we run. "We're gonna get soaked," she says as I pull even with her.

We race past the IMAGINATION, HONESTY, and DILIGENCE trash bins, across the footbridge with its hollow thump and down the slippery path, past the Oarweed restaurant and through the parking lot, and the rain lets loose with amazing power just as we duck under the green-and-white awning by the ice-cream place. It's late enough that everything is closed, even the Hurricane, so we're the only ones here. Lightning is flashing everywhere, and the boats are bouncing around in the cove. Her shoulder presses against mine as we try to stay dry.

The rain is incredibly hard and it's blowing straight toward the ocean, so the awning overhead isn't doing us much good. But it all smells clean and briny and cold, and there's a huge crash of thunder and the lights in the cove go out, so it's pitch black and drenching and there's hail mixing in with the rain.

She takes my hand and pulls me around the corner of the shop, underneath the steps that lead up to an art gallery, and pushes open a low wooden door. We duck down into a shedlike storage area. "We used to take our breaks down here when I was an ice-cream scooper," she says. "Me and Faith would hide down here and eat Gummi Bears."

We wait a few seconds for our eyes to adjust. "Good," she says, pointing to a plastic chaise lounge in the corner of the tiny space. "It's still here." She shuts the door and slips a hand under my shirt, lifting it to my chin and over my head and off. "This'll be a million times more comfortable than those rocks we were on anyway."

I lie on the chaise and she climbs on top of me and we pick up right where we left off.

The rain has stopped when we cautiously emerge, but the wind is blowing hard and the sky is clear overhead with thousands of stars. The storm has blown out to sea, and there's lightning on the horizon. The electricity is still off, but we can see all right.

We head for the public bathrooms at the far end of the cove, marked BUOYS and GULLS.

I try to keep the bathroom door open with my foot to let some light in, but my leg is about seven feet too short. So I take a mental picture, make some estimated steps toward the urinal, and release.

The storm has scattered some of the garbage piled outside Barnacle Billy's. Mercy says they serve more than a thousand lobsters a day in the high season.

"How many does your place do?"

"Maybe a hundred."

"Are you supposed to get home sometime?" I ask.

She shakes her head. "I told them I was staying at a friend's."

We walk up the hill toward town. "What time is it, you think?"

"I have no idea," she says. "After three."

It turns out that it's quarter to four when we reach the apartment. "You wanna crash for a while?" I ask.

"Yeah."

So we shake out the blanket and curl up on the couch. Jack comes home about eight thirty and we sit up in a hurry.

"Hey, kids," he says with a smirk.

"Hi," she says. "Have a nice night?"

"I did. You, too?"

She looks at me and smiles. "It was great. We got caught in that storm and had to wait it out in the cove."

"Sounds like fun. You guys want coffee?"

She thinks it over, then says, "No thanks."

"I guess I don't, either," he says. "Probably should crash for a couple of hours. Didn't get a whole lot of sleep."

I still don't know who his mystery woman is. Probably somebody who hangs out at the bar.

"We'll bolt," I say. "Let you get some sleep. I'm hungry anyway."

"You won't bother me."

"No problem. I'll buy some breakfast for once."

"That's the rule," he says. He winks at me, intending for her to see it, too. "If a date lasts till morning, you gotta buy her some food."

I'm not very hungry, since we had those sandwiches in the middle of the night, but I want to get out of the apartment. So we leave.

She gets another bag of chocolate-covered almonds—dark ones this time—from the Harbor Candy Shop. Then we backtrack to the gelato place, which also has pastries and teas and coffee.

She gets an espresso and I get some coconut gelato, and we sit on a bench in front of Fancy That and eat our unusual breakfast.

The street is busy with walkers crinkling open their white paper bags from Bread & Roses Bakery, eating cinnamon sticks and muffins, getting crumbs on the brick sidewalk.

A guy on the bench next to us is doing crisis management via his cell phone. "Marissa? Hi! It's Jeffrey. From Workout World? I'm afraid I have to cancel our session. . . . Yeah, I got called out of town and it couldn't be helped. But I'll definitely see you on Friday."

He's a good-looking guy, very fit. Obviously he stayed over in Ogunquit unexpectedly. He's sitting next to the guy he spent the night with.

Mercy leans into me and whispers teasingly, "You're staring at him."

"Am not."

"Are too."

I turn to her. She's laughing. "I think I proved myself," I say, puffing out my chest.

She grabs my bicep and squeezes.

He makes a second call. "Janet? It's Jeffrey. . . . I'm great. Listen, I need a favor. It's my eleven o'clock aerobics class. The guy who was supposed to cover for me called and cancelled. I was already in *Maine* when he called. Is there any way you could teach it?" He puts his hand over the phone and turns to his buddy. "Oh my God. She goes, 'Would I have to put on a jockstrap?' Hilarious." He puts the phone back to his ear. "Oh my God, Janet, you are the best! I love you!"

A flabby bald guy jogs past in a headband and madras shorts.

All the straight people start jogging when they get up here. Eleven and a half months of sitting on their butts at home, then they get the inspiration to turn it around in a week.

"So now what?" Mercy asks.

"What?"

"This schedule . . . We can't stay up every night."

"You would *want* to?"

"I want to be with you. As much as I can, at least."

"Me, too."

"Summer goes fast."

"We'll find time."

She pats my leg. "Not as much as we'd like."

"I'll get a night off now and then. They don't own me."

"Believe me, they think they *do* own us for the summer. They have to bleed every minute they can from their places when it's hot. Nobody's making any money around here in January."

"Still. We could ask for one night off."

"Yeah, well I'm out by nine thirty every night. Your job is the problem."

"I have to work."

"I know." She glances at Jeffrey and his friend on the other bench, then looks at her shoes. "I just don't like the idea that my primary rival gets access to you every night of the week."

"You mean Hector?"

"Yeah. I do."

I let out my breath and look at the sky. "You're still stuck on that?"

She shrugs. "I see him looking at you."

"So what? Am I looking back?"

"Don't get angry."

"I'm not gay."

"Okay. I believe you. But can't you see where I'm coming from? I just met you. You work in a gay bar."

"Yeah, I *work* there. That doesn't make me gay."

"Okay, and being wary doesn't make me some homophobic monster, either. I told you what happened at school."

Arnie's walking toward us with Caruso leading the way. Haven't seen him in a few days, or nights.

"Hey, Arnie."

"Hello."

Mercy kneels down to pet Caruso. "How you doing, boy?"

"He hasn't been well," Arnie says. He looks exhausted.

"What's wrong?" I ask.

"They think it might be cancer."

"No." Caruso's a young dog. Seems really vibrant. I bend down and pet him, too. "What happened?"

"He couldn't keep anything down, so I took him to the vet. We're waiting for some results, but it doesn't look good."

"Shit." I stand up. Arnie's crying. I put my hand on his shoulder. He seems frail.

"This is as far as we've walked in a week," he says. "I'll probably have to carry him back."

I bend down next to Mercy again and gently rub Caruso's snout. He looks the same to me. He starts sniffing my hand and wagging his tail. "Hope you're okay," I say. "You're a good boy, aren't you?"

"He's the best," Arnie says. "All he ever wants is a walk and his dinner. Never complains, he's never naughty."

I stand. "Keep us posted. We miss you over at Dishes."

"I'll stop in soon," he says. "I just haven't wanted to leave him alone."

"I know what you mean."

He's a good little dog. Hope he's okay. For his sake and for Arnie's.

"So sad," Mercy says as we start walking again.

"It sucks."

We stop and look back. Some little kids are petting Caruso.

Mercy puts her arm around me.

"Hector's not your rival," I say.

"I think maybe he is."

"He can't be unless I was interested, right? And I'm not."

"That's good." She squeezes my shoulder. "Because if you were, he'd be on you in a second."

# 10

## "He couldn't reach his shoulder blades."

Chase comes in during a lull. Just what I need. He hoists himself onto the metal prep table and sits there with his feet dangling. "Could you put some cream on my shoulders?" he asks.

I give him an incredulous look, which I've been practicing a lot lately. "What?"

"I got sunburned on the beach." He's pulling up the sleeve of his T-shirt to show me a patch of pink skin. "It's nasty."

There's a pump bottle of CVS Total Moisture lotion on the shelf above the sink. I use it sometimes; you keep your hands in dishwater all night and you need it.

He looks at me hopefully. "Okay?"

I frown but say, "Yeah."

He peels off his shirt and stands with his back to me. "Careful," he says. "Do it soft."

I pump some lotion into my palm and smear it above his shoulder blade and toward his arm. Then I do the other side.

Of course, that's when Mercy sticks her head in from the back door. "Hello?" she says.

I turn to her and keep rubbing. "Come on in," I say. "We're just caressing each other."

"Sounds like fun." She's wearing a black Adidas top, zipped to the chest.

Chase steps away and smiles at me. "That was great," he says. "Am I really scorched back there?"

"You'll live."

"Thanks, Danny." He puts the shirt back on and turns to Mercy. "He has nice strong hands."

She gives him a hard look. "Tell me about it."

Chase leaves.

"That looked cozy," Mercy says.

"He got sunburned."

"I could tell."

"So what are you up to?"

"Just thought I'd see how you were doing."

"Got a long way to go," I say. "Like, three more hours, at least."

"Can you take a break?"

"Yeah."

We step outside. "I brought you something," she says, pulling a cellophane bag of red licorice wheels from her pocket.

I take one and chew it. "You eat a lot of candy, huh?"

"My parents never let us have it."

I lean against the wall and she leans into me.

"Checking up on me?" I ask.

I feel her shrug. "I guess. . . . All those rivals."

I think she's kidding this time. I kiss her forehead. "I'm all yours," I say.

"Can I take a nap in your apartment?" she asks.

I lean away from her. "Yeah. How come?"

"So I'll be there when you get home. Sound good?"

"Sounds great."

She takes my right hand in both of hers and starts rubbing my fingers. Her voice is teasing but also has a bit of an edge: "Nice and *strong.*"

I feel myself blush. "He couldn't reach his shoulder blades."

"Good thing *you* could."

"He practically begged me."

"They'll do that."

Mercy climbs up to sit on the prep table. "You know what's funny?" she says. "My parents are so controlling, and yours are so . . ."

"Out of touch?"

She tilts her head to the side. "Sounds like it. As parents, I mean. But here I am—an *adult*—and I sneak candy and lie to my parents about where I go at night. How dysfunctional is that? At least your dad treats you as an equal."

"Maybe *too* equal sometimes."

"Somewhere there ought to be a balance. I don't think any of our parents really get that."

She leaves a few minutes later—with my key—because the less time I spend with her now the quicker I'll get out of here. She said she'd straighten up the apartment for us, but I don't think there's much of a mess.

Jack tells me to haul some cases of beer and wine upstairs. Sal winks at me as I'm lugging up a case of Corona. "Hey, there"— he's singing with the piano crowd, gazing at me—"you with the stars in your eyes. . . ."

I give him an embarrassed smile. All of the tables are full and the crowd around the piano is at least three deep. It's an easy place to hook up with someone, but Sal never seems to have any luck.

Hector still seems sort of downcast. He comes in about twelve thirty and tells me things are slowing down.

"That's good," I say. "I'm hoping to get out of here on time."

"I might leave early," he says, staring toward the door into the bar room. "I don't feel like seeing who *Chase* leaves with."

"It won't be you?"

"*Definitely* not me." Hector swallows hard. "Apparently he's had enough of me already."

I go to the door and look toward the bar. Chase must be upstairs; there's still a sizable crowd up there. Downstairs Jack has only four people at the bar—three of them together staring at the television set and a young dark-haired woman down the other end. Pretty damn cute to be sitting there alone.

"Chase is a bit of a whore, isn't he?" I say to Hector.

"I wouldn't quite say that."

"He seems to get around, though."

Hector takes off his apron and sets it on the table. "Those first couple of nights he was here were so . . . God!" He shakes his head and frowns. "Next thing I know, like *that*"—he snaps his fingers—"he's leaving the bar with some guy from New *Hamp-shire*, for God's sake. He said it was nothing. Two nights in a *row* it was nothing? I don't think so."

"Yeah, well, we all have problems. I finally meet this great-looking girl and she thinks I'm in denial about my sexuality."

"She does?"

"Well, she did. Seems to be over it finally."

"She is or you?"

I give a snorty laugh. "I convinced her."

"I thought Chase would be my great summer romance," he says. "I mean, we talked online all spring and couldn't wait to see each other. Then he gets here and it lasts about five seconds."

He looks down at the floor and then back up at me, hesitating before speaking again. "I think you and I are both looking for the same thing. Somebody who . . . wants us and isn't playing psycho-logical games."

I lean against the sink and fold my arms. I hear what he's saying. We're right here in front of each other and all we have to do is reach. "I guess it's never easy," I say. But my reach doesn't extend that far.

Chase walks in. Hector walks right past him toward the bar.

Chase watches him go, then gives me an amused look. "In a hurry, isn't he?"

"Not too much," I say. "He's not in a rush. Like some people."

Chase gives a huffy laugh with the corner of his mouth turned up. Then he starts singing again. "Summertime . . ." He flicks his eyebrows up at me. "I didn't come here to get married."

I make a last haul from the bar and Jack puts his hand on my shoulder. "Want you to meet someone," he says.

The woman at the end of the bar—she's older than me but probably not more than twenty-five—smiles at me as I walk over.

"Danny, this is Sonia," Jack says.

I shake her hand. She blushes a bit and says, "Pleasure to meet you." She's got one of those Eastern-Bloc accents and red lipstick. Like I said, she's gorgeous.

I look at Jack. His gentle smirk affirms that they're together.

"You live here?" I ask.

She looks at Jack, then smiles at me again. "Six months," she says. She turns her gaze to Jack. "Maybe longer."

"Maybe a *lot* longer," he says.

There's one of those blue Saratoga water bottles on the bar. Jack picks it up and refills her glass, which has a big wedge of lime in it and some ice cubes.

"Almost done in there?" Jack asks me.

"Getting close." I lean slightly toward him and lower my voice. "Mercy's at the house."

He nods. "We won't walk in on you." He puts his hand over Sonia's and looks at her. "We've got plans for the rest of the night. Sonia's got a nice room in a boardinghouse."

"No roommate?" I ask.

"Not this year," she says. "Other years there were two or three or four of us. Finally I have some . . . autonomy?"

"Autonomy's a good thing," I say. I pick up the tray of used glasses and say good night.

Poor Hector is back in the kitchen. I load the dishwasher one last time and start wiping down the counters.

I hear him sigh. "You busy?"

"A few more minutes," I say.

"No. I mean after."

I turn and nod slowly. "Yeah." I say it like I mean it, which I do.

"Oh."

"I'm meeting somebody."

"That girl?"

"Yeah. Why? What's up?"

"Just thought you might come over for a drink with us or something." He waves off the thought. "Just wanted to ask."

"Thanks. She's waiting."

"It's okay." He smiles bravely. "You have a good time, okay?"

"I will. Don't . . . Another night, all right? Really."

He seems to brighten up. "Okay. You have fun. . . . Tell her I said hello."

"I'll do that."

He goes out the back door, avoiding Chase.

It takes me about fifteen minutes to finish up. Hector comes back as I'm leaving—fresh shirt (the black one that he loaned me), fresh hair gel, fresh shot of cologne.

"He just left," I say. I'd seen Chase leaving with a group of four or five customers about three minutes ago.

"I don't care," Hector says. "Could you tell where they were going?"

"No. I was in here."

"Well, it's either Five-O or the Porch," he says. "Hopefully we'll pick the other one."

Not sure who "we" are. I could ask, but I don't. I've got better things on my mind. Mercy's waiting.

# 11

## "So get your frickin' hand off me."

We wake up early and shower together. Fortunately there's a new bar of soap and a bottle of cheap shampoo. Then she makes us peanut-butter sandwiches and we walk out on the Marginal Way.

There's a light drizzle, so the path is much less crowded than usual. Even at eight a.m. there'd be a steady stream of people. The rain is little more than a cool mist. It feels great on the skin.

A couple of kayakers in bright red are paddling hard to get clear of the river. The rough surf is a shiny, choppy gray.

When she sleeps, Mercy lets out a quiet but distinct nasally snore every once in a while. On her lower back she has a reddish birth mark the size of a potato chip and shaped something like a map of Mexico.

Dozens of cairns have appeared on the shore since yesterday—piles of flattish, round rocks, hockey-puck to football sized. Mercy says it's a legitimate art form.

A gull flies over the rocks and drops a mussel from about thirty feet up. The bird lands and starts picking at the meat from the broken shells, and a couple of others scramble over, squawking and trying to steal it.

We stop and watch the gulls for several minutes. Mercy's the first woman I've ever slept an entire night with, first I've ever showered with, first who ever really seemed to like me.

A lobster boat goes churning by, heading for Perkins Cove.

Somehow I keep beating the odds.


The bar's been busy and the evening goes quickly.

I'm scrubbing some pans around midnight when Chase walks in.

"Shoulders feel great," he says to me. "Thanks again for rubbing them last night."

"Okay."

He puts his hands on my shoulders and starts massaging. "I could return the favor."

"No need to."

He pushes a little harder. "The night's almost over," he whispers. "It'd be my pleasure."

I shrug his hands away. "What, are you kidding me?"

He starts that annoying song again. "Summertime . . ."

I turn back to the sink. "No way."

"You're not even a teensy bit curious?"

"Not even that much."

"Well, I hope you're at least flattered that I'd suggest it."

I turn again and feel my blood rushing to the surface. "You screw around with every guy who walks in here."

"I do *not*."

"Seems that way."

"Not even close," he says. "Do you have any idea how many men hit on me every night?"

"No idea."

"A *lot*."

Hector's in the kitchen now, too. "A lot of what?" he asks.

"A lot of nerve." I wince a little when I say it—sounds like something my grandmother would say.

Hector sizes up the situation pretty quick. He glares at Chase. "Can't control yourself, can you?"

Chase laughs. "Take a Midol."

Hector takes a step forward and puts his hand on Chase's chest, giving him a little shove. "You *are* a whore, aren't you?"

"What do you care?"

"I *don't*. I did for a while, like a stupid jerk."

"So get your frickin' hand off me."

Hector pushes again. Chase takes a step back, then brings up both hands and shoves Hector harder.

Hector grabs Chase's shoulders and they start pushing back and forth. Hector calls Chase an asshole. Chase calls Hector a pansy.

"Take it outside," I say. I don't mind seeing them fight, but with the metal sinks and the knives and the damp floor, somebody might get hurt.

I follow them out the back door and they start punching. We're only a matter of feet from Shore Road, so a small crowd gathers in a hurry. It's mostly a wrestling match, too close for any fully swinging punches.

I hear a bicycle clatter to the sidewalk and a cop breaks through the crowd, yelling at Hector and Chase to back off.

They step apart. Hector adjusts his shirt, which is pulled up to his ear on one side. Chase is feeling inside his mouth with his thumb. He spits out some bloody saliva.

Mercy suddenly appears and nudges my arm. She sounds a little giddy. "They fighting over you?"

I don't answer.

I hear the outside steps rattling and see Sal coming down as quickly as he can. An actual bouncer situation! Kyle and Sergei are looking out that door, and several others are at the down-stairs exit.

The cop very politely asks the crowd to move along. He asks Sal if he's the manager and Sal says no.

Fitch left hours ago. Jack steps out and says that he's in charge tonight. The cop waves him over, and they stand there talking with Hector and Chase.

Jack juts his thumb toward the building a couple of times, making eye contact with Kyle and me and the others. Sal stays out there with his hand on Hector's shoulder.

Mercy follows me into the kitchen. I look into the downstairs bar room and see that Bernie has come down to take over.

"What was that about?" Mercy asks.

"Just bullshit. Chase hits on everybody, right in Hector's face."

"Hector needs to get over it."

Jack walks in, shaking his head and grinning at Mercy. "Boys," he says.

"They get arrested?" I ask.

"Nooooo. I smoothed it over."

"They still out there?"

"I told Chase to stay upstairs the rest of the night. Hector went home to get cleaned up. He can work down here."

"So that's it?"

"For now. Fitch can sort it out tomorrow. I mean, shit, that was nothing. It'll blow over in five minutes. . . . What the hell happened anyway?"

I shrug. "Bad breakup, I guess."

Jack laughs. "Hector should know better than that. No *way* he was going to get Chase to be loyal all summer."

"How would he know?"

"They both worked here last year; Hector knew the story."

Mercy has her arm around me. "Hector needs somebody true," she says. "He's a romantic."

Jack's still grinning. "Hector's a nut." He pushes open the door and goes back to the bar.

I hug Mercy. "So what are you doing here?" I ask.

"Stalking you."

"That's nice."

"Actually, I'm tired as hell. Thought I'd walk up here and say good night and get some decent sleep for a change."

"Okay," I say. "Maybe tomorrow night?"

"Yeah." She kisses me hard. "You get some sleep, too. No going out with your boyfriends."

"But I have so many to choose from."

"They got nothing on me," she whispers. "I've got everything you need."

She kisses me even harder, then pulls away with a playful smile. "Oh, shit," she says. "Maybe a couple more hours won't kill me." She hops her butt onto the prep table. "So why were they fighting?"

"Chase was hitting on me."

"Oh, God." She shakes her head. "See what I said?"

I shrug. "It was nothing. It was more about them than about me."

So she hangs around and watches me finish up. I'm wringing out the mop when Jack sticks his head into the kitchen. "I'm buying," he says. "You guys up for it?"

"Sure."

The place is closed and there's just one light on in the bar room. It's empty except for Hector, Sal, and Sonia, who are sitting at a booth across from the bar. Jack's at the bar with a pitcher. "Shipyard okay with everybody?" he asks.

He comes to the booth and pours six glasses of beer, then goes back and refills the pitcher.

He slides in next to Sonia. Sal's against the wall on Hector's side. I move a chair over from a table and sit at the end with Mercy on my lap.

"Quite an evening," Jack says with a smirk.

Hector is slumped back a bit, looking sort of dazed. "He's a prick," he says softly.

"You got in a few good shots," Jack says. "He was bleeding."

Hector just sighs and runs his finger around the rim of his beer glass.

I look at Sonia, huddled in the corner of the booth. She smiles back, then pokes Jack in the arm with a finger. "The bloodiest is the loser?" she says.

Jack shakes his head. "Not always. Whoever's left standing."

Sal is drumming two fingers tunelessly on the table. I take a swig of the beer and it feels cold and malty going down my throat. My shirt is damp and smells like dishwater. I go back to the kitchen for a dry one.

When I return Hector has his back against Sal and is slumped a bit more. His eyes are closed.

"So, Danny and Mercy," Sonia says, "you are going well?"

"Yeah." I glance at Hector. He shuts his eyes slightly tighter. "We met a couple of weeks ago."

"That was quick."

"I guess."

I refill my glass and look at Jack. "Any munchies?" I ask.

He waves toward the bar. "Go get 'em."

Mercy gets up and finds a bag of chips and a jar of peanuts.

Hector sits up and takes a handful of the nuts. "I'm starving."

"Fighting'll do that, Rocky," Sal says.

Hector makes that scolding sound. "It lasted about three seconds."

"More than that," I say. "You guys were at it for a good minute before that cop came by."

"It had to be at least that long," Sal says. "Kyle comes running out of the kitchen yelling, 'Fight! Fight!' My heart just about jumped out of my throat."

"You must have been moving pretty quick," Jack says to Sal. "I heard the stairs shaking—thought the side of the building was caving in."

Sal blushes and grins and wipes his forehead with his palm. "I can move when I have to, but don't get in my way when I've got momentum. There's no telling if I can stop."

"Good thing you didn't get there too quickly," Hector says, smiling now. He sits up, eyes open. "He was winning for the first few seconds, then I smacked him pretty good."

"You hurt your hand?" Jack asks.

"Less than I hurt his face." Hector lifts his hand triumphantly and makes a fist. "Felt pretty good, I have to admit. The son of a bitch deserved it."

# 12

## "Doesn't look quite so pretty."

By ten the next morning the cars are already backed up as far as you can see coming into town. Crowds of people are waiting outside the few restaurants that serve breakfast. And every bench is filled in front of Fancy That.

Jack and Sonia are at one of the metal tables with coffee and doughnuts. I'm dripping wet from my run, but I do have a shirt on, so I go over and sit down.

"How's things at home?" Jack says with a grin. He hasn't slept there all week.

"Lonely."

"No." He knows I've got a regular visitor.

"Not really."

"Maybe we'll stay there tonight." Jack looks at Sonia. She shrugs. "Maybe we need a bigger place," he says. "Get you a bedroom."

"I'm okay on the couch," I say.

"Yeah, but for how long? You're sticking around this fall, right?"

"You want me to?"

"Damn right I do."

"Then it looks like I should stay."

Jack picks up Sonia's wrist and gently twists it around, showing me that she's wearing a ring with a small diamond in it.

She wiggles her fingers at me. "Like it?"

I'm confused, but I say, "Yeah."

Jack raises his eyebrows and looks at me like I'm an idiot. "It's an engagement ring."

"Oh . . . congratulations."

They both laugh.

"Kind of sudden," I say.

"Gotta get around her visa," Jack says. "We get married, she doesn't have to go back to Bulgaria. If we don't, she's gone in September."

"That would suck, huh?"

Jack nods. "It would definitely suck. It was a painful winter last year. We don't want to go through that again."

So obviously they started this thing a year ago. I didn't know that. But I've also been thinking about me and Mercy. She goes back to Boston before Labor Day. My plans are still somewhat liquid.

"So," Jack says, "we're thinking we could rent a house in October. They're dirt cheap around here until May. What do you think?"

"That'd be good."

"We're going up to Portland to see an immigration lawyer on Monday," Jack says. "He said on the phone this'll probably work."

"So no Florida trip this winter?"

"Nah. I can tend bar up here or in Boston."

"Time to settle down, huh?"

Sonia shakes her head and laughs. "This guy?"

"I'll settle," he says, patting her on the head. He winks at me. "She's the first person who ever made me *want* to settle down."

"And he's quitting smoking," Sonia says.

"*Try*ing to," Jack says.

"So when's the wedding?"

"As soon as it has to be," Jack says. "We'll see what the lawyer thinks." He looks at her, and he's beaming. "It might be Monday afternoon, for all I know."

"Guess I should buy a tie."

"I'll loan you one. But it probably won't be till August. . . . Anyway, we're gonna celebrate tonight after work. Squeeze as many as we can into the apartment."

"That'll be about six people."

"Yeah. If two of them stand on the deck."

So that's a lot to think about as I walk back. Sonia seems nice and all, but we've probably said nine words to each other. We're gonna be this big happy family all of a sudden?

I stop and look at a poster advertising the Mr. Ogunquit Contest, next Saturday on the beach. And there's a sign on the door of the Front Porch saying TRY OUR NEW BEEFCAKE SALAD!

Arnie is across the street with Caruso, talking to the guy who runs the art gallery. They're both laughing, and Caruso seems to be chewing something. So I go over.

I nod to the men and kneel down to pet Caruso. He starts licking my hand and wagging his tail. "How you doing, boy? How you doing?"

"He's much better," Arnie says.

I look up. "Good results?"

Arnie starts to speak, then chokes up and wipes his eyes. But he's nodding his head. "Very good," he says.

"Not cancer?"

"No. Thank God. He's eating again, too. Whatever was wrong seems to have passed."


I go in to work early, mostly out of curiosity. Hector is setting tables in the dining room; Jack is hooking up a new keg of beer; no sign of Chase.

"So did Fitch say anything?" I ask Hector.

He shakes his head but says, "He called us in about an hour ago. Just goes, 'You guys cool?' I go, '*I* am.'"

"What'd Chase say?"

"He said it was nothing." Hector grins. "He's got a purple, puffy lip. Doesn't look quite so pretty today."

"So that was it?"

"Yeah. You think Fitch hasn't had to deal with complaints from the cops before? This is a bar."

He follows me into the kitchen. I take a trash bag I overlooked last night out to the Dumpster, walking past the site of the famous battle. Hector stays with me.

"I hear we're coming to your place after work?" he asks.

"My place?"

"You and your *dad.*"

"Yeah. The big celebration."

"That's wild that they're getting married."

I open the Dumpster lid and toss in the bag. The smell of rotting garbage makes me want to spit.

"Why'd you keep that quiet?" he asks.

"That they're getting married? I had no idea."

"No. About you and Jack."

"I don't know," I say. "He thought I'd fit in better, I guess."

"Think it worked?"

"Probably. You guys might have treated me different."

"Might have. . . . Never would have thought in a million years that he was somebody's father."

"Why not?"

Hector rolls his eyes. He crinkles up his mouth like he's weighing his words, then says, "*He* kind of acts like a kid."

"Yeah, well"—I spread my palms and hold them up—"I guess we all grow up sometime."

"So," he says, "is *she* coming to the party?"

"Sonia?"

"Mercy."

"Yeah."

"So it's going better with her now?"

"It's been good. Really good." I take a few steps away from the Dumpster and take a seat on the bottom of the outside steps.

"That's great, Danny," he says.

"You think?"

"Of course I do. Why wouldn't I?"

*Because you had other ideas.* But Hector seems like his old self—more than his old self. Confident. Upbeat. The fight did him a lot of good.

"I was afraid you might be jealous," I say.

His eyes get wide. "Oh, come on. No."

"Not at all?"

He blushes and looks away with an embarrassed smile. "Not anymore." He reaches for my hair and brushes a few strands off my forehead. "Does every relationship have to be sexual? Just because we're *friendly*, because we can talk and joke around, that doesn't mean I want you like that."

He puts his hand on my shoulder and gives me a motherly look. "*Dan*-ny. Danny, Danny, Danny. You're *so* straight. So, so, *so*, so straight. . . . You still think we want to sleep with every guy we meet, don't you?"

"No. I don't think that at all."

"You thought I wanted to sleep with *you*."

"Didn't you?"

He motions for me to shove over, then sits next to me on the step. "Maybe," he says softly. "I guess a part of me did."

"And which part would that be?"

He makes that scolding sound and grins. "My *brain*, thank you." Then he turns serious and looks away. "Didn't you?"

"Didn't I what?"

He clears his throat and turns to me again. "You can't say you weren't attracted."

"Can't I?"

"Not if you're being honest with yourself."

I fold my arms and lean way forward, looking at the pavement. "Okay," I say slowly. "Not . . . physically, so much as emotionally. I mean . . . I *like* you. Like you said, it isn't always sexual." I can feel my face turning red with embarrassment. "Maybe we both misinterpreted."

"You're a *really* nice guy," he tells me.

"So are you."

"You deserve a great partner."

I sit up and turn to face him.

He raises his eyebrows. "A *female* one. Okay?"

"You deserve one, too," I say. "Whatever kind you want."

"Okay." He pats my thigh. "It's behind us. We can kiss and make up." He leans toward me with his lips pursed, then pulls back and laughs. And he puts on this teasing, gently sarcastic voice. "It's o-*kay* to be straight, honey. Really, it is. You were just born that way. You can't help it."

My face gets even warmer, but I smile. "Nice of you to say that."

Now he's really riding me. "I know it's hard to be so different in an environment like this, where everybody's so theatrical and prancy, but we all understand, Danny. You're just wired differently than the rest of us. So go"—he waves his hand toward the street— "go out there and play football and change a carburetor and shoot a deer. We'll still love you. Because we *care*."

"Thanks. That's very sweet of you."

He stands and gives me an exaggerated, loose-wristed hand

flap as he heads toward the kitchen. "I love you, Danny," he says. "Just not *that* way. Sorry."

He stops at the door. "And by way," he says, "I think I might have found what I deserve."

About a dozen of us cram into the apartment. Jack opens three bottles of champagne and announces that the wedding will be on the Marginal Way. "Labor Day weekend or sometime before," he says. "We'll definitely keep you all posted."

Shy, quiet Sal says he wants to make a toast, holding his glass up and clearing his throat. It's a song, but he speaks it. "Somewhere, over the rainbow . . ." He beams at Jack and Sonia. People are laughing about the Judy Garland selection, but what else would Sal come up with? He goes on with the rest of the song— about daring to dream and bluebirds flying and all that.

Everyone claps. I laugh, too, but my eyes tear up. Mercy squeezes my shoulders from behind.

I shake Sal's hand. "Nice toast," I say.

He looks down and blushes. "It's all true," he says softly. "Those words can break your heart. But they can also keep you going."

He looks up and smiles at Hector, who's smiling sweetly back.

Mercy pushes me down on the couch and sits on my lap. "*Two* romantics," she whispers in my ear.

"Them?" I ask, whispering back.

"Of course, them," she says. "You didn't see that coming?"

"Not in a billion years."

"Well, this universe has been around for *fourteen* billion years. The odds are definitely in their favor. . . . Why do you think Sal ran so fast down the stairs the other night?"

I shrug. "To save the day?"

She smiles.

"They're so . . . different," I say. Sal is twice as big as Hector and dresses like an old man.

"No," she says. "They're exactly the same inside. Why shouldn't two kind people be together?"

I dump my champagne and find a Coke in the back of the refrigerator, straining to keep my eyes open. We go out on the deck and she leans with her back against the railing. I lean into her.

"I am *dead* tired," she says. "And I have to be at work in six hours."

I look back into the apartment. It's quarter to five, but they're still packed in there. "Not much chance of getting any sleep here."

"Can you walk me home?"

"Sure."

We go in to get our sweatshirts. I kiss Sonia on the cheek and give Jack a hug. He's been gnawing on an unlit cigar for at least an hour, but he says he'll never smoke another one. People start talking about heading out when they notice that me and Mercy are leaving.

Hector, Sal, Kyle, and Bernie follow us down the steps. Kyle and Bernie cross the street, Sal and Hector make a right, and we make the left up Shore Road.

I look back after half a block. Sal and Hector are holding hands. I put my arm more tightly around Mercy. "Hey, I think I can sneak out at midnight tonight."

"I don't know, Danny. I think I'll be asleep way before then."

"No problem." I yawn. "Time for me to catch up, too."

We stop in front of her house, a red clapboarded Cape a few doors up from the fire station.

"You glad they're getting married?" she asks.

"I guess. You never know with my dad. How long he'll stick, I mean."

"I think he loves her."

"I think so, too."

She gives me a long kiss and runs her hand firmly along the back of my neck. "Love's a funny thing," she says. "It happens in surprising places."

I walk along Shore Road and cut up through the cemetery, past all the Maxwells and Littlefields and Hartwells, and over the hill toward the Marginal Way. I seem to be the only person out this early.

It's not quite sunrise yet. The breeze is coming off the ocean and the tide is high, sending a moist spray toward me as I climb onto the rocks and take a seat.

The brightest stars are still visible as the sky begins to lighten out by the horizon. Some tough little sea roses above me are giving off a faint flowery aroma. And the surf keeps going in and out, never hesitating. Feels as if my heartbeat falls into that same rhythm almost immediately.

I run my thumb deeply along my thigh, feeling the slight soreness from all those hills I've been running. And when I stretch my arms overhead and take in a long, slow breath, I feel invigorated—so physical and alive.

I *would* be here, somehow. I know that. There can't be just that one opportunity, that one race to the goal that either makes you who you are or knocks you out of the running forever.

I inch farther down the rocks, closer to the sea, that force that animates us all. A gull wings over the surf. A wave breaks hard against the rocks. A warning buoy down near the cove flashes red, and the sun begins to poke above the horizon.

I inhale again, deeper than I ever have, and fill my lungs with the spray of the ocean, the mixture of plant and fish and salt and energy and strength and spirit and desire.

If you can imagine what the beginning of life would smell like, I have to believe it'd be this.

**Rich Wallace** was a high school and college athlete and then a sportswriter before he began writing novels. He is the author of many critically acclaimed sports-themed novels, including *Wrestling Sturbridge*, *Restless: A Ghost's Story*, and *One Good Punch*, as well as the Winning Season series. Wallace lives with his family in Honesdale, Pennsylvania.